Use your time wisely.

Lauren didn't need to hear the words echoing ominously between them.

She *shouldn't* be excited by this game. She dealt in the practical, the tangible, not the whimsical. And yet...something about the gauntlet Tahir had thrown sparked something within her.

Something she'd be wise not to give in to.

So what if she'd thrived on challenges once upon a time? This time with Tahir was far from a fairy tale.

After that much-needed reminder to herself, she rose from her seat, tugging the stole firmly around her.

"Where do you think you're going?"

She paused, unwilling to admit his deep, rumbling voice triggered another micro-tsunami within her. Neutralizing her expression, she turned. "You've explained the rules and I've agreed to play your game. I'm assuming you'll fit me in at some point tomorrow?"

"You're mistaken. The game will be over by this time tomorrow."

She stiffened. "What do you mean?"

"It means you only have twenty-four hours with me in the desert to earn my consideration. And your time started fifteen minutes ago when you entered my tent."

Brothers of the Desert

Born to rule. Ruled by temptation!

Desert royals Tahir and Javid have a lot to do if they plan to propel the kingdom of Jukarat into the world arena as a superpower. But being heirs to a powerful nation on the rise is no easy feat... Especially when passion becomes part of the equation!

Bound by duty, the brothers have always put their nation first, but the pull of the forbidden is something neither could have predicted. And soon it becomes just as important as the throne they were born to protect...

Read Tahir and Lauren's story in
Their Desert Night of Scandal
Available now!

And read Javid and Anais's story
Coming soon!

Maya Blake

—

THEIR DESERT NIGHT OF SCANDAL

Recycling programs for this product may not exist in your area.

ISBN-13: 978-1-335-58382-6

Their Desert Night of Scandal

Harlequin Enterprises ULC
22 Adelaide St. West, 41st Floor
Toronto, Ontario M5H 4E3, Canada
www.Harlequin.com

Printed in U.S.A.

Maya Blake's hopes of becoming a writer were born when she picked up her first romance at thirteen. Little did she know her dream would come true! Does she still pinch herself every now and then to make sure it's not a dream? Yes, she does! Feel free to pinch her, too, via Twitter, Facebook or Goodreads! Happy reading!

Books by Maya Blake

Harlequin Presents

The Sicilian's Banished Bride
The Commanding Italian's Challenge
The Greek's Hidden Vows
Reclaimed for His Royal Bed

Passion in Paradise

Kidnapped for His Royal Heir

The Notorious Greek Billionaires

Claiming My Hidden Son
Bound by My Scandalous Pregnancy

Ghana's Most Eligible Billionaires

Bound by Her Rival's Baby
A Vow to Claim His Hidden Son

Visit the Author Profile page
at Harlequin.com for more titles.

CHAPTER ONE

SHEIKH TAHIR BIN HALIM AL-JUKRAT had dealt with his most senior aide long enough to know the older man's tells. Yet Ali insisted on playing these games with him. Tahir watched him fidget with the papers in his leather-bound folder, straighten corners that didn't need straightening, place the expensive Montblanc pen Tahir had gifted him two Christmases ago precisely in the centre of the top page before moving it a fraction of an inch.

Given the chance, Tahir suspected the other man would've conducted a microscopic inspection of each fingernail for dirt and brushed invisible lint off his tailored suit before stating what was obviously on his mind.

'Are we done here? I'd like to get on with my next appointment before I leave for Zinabir,' Tahir said after a full minute, attempting and failing to keep impatience from sharpening his voice.

Ali gave the merest grimace, an action not many would've noticed.

Tahir noticed.

He noticed everything. Because these days, he couldn't afford to be oblivious to anything. Not any more.

Those carefree days when he'd freely trusted, and tossed out benefits of the doubt like candy at a toddler's party, were far behind him. Smothered to death by a far too close brush with a different fate. A fate averted at a steep price he'd never be able to fully repay in this life.

In his quietest moments, Tahir couldn't help but hope he would be able to repay it in his next. Hoped to have done enough in this life to erase the deep disappointment from his father's eyes when they met in the afterlife.

Until then…

He tightened his gut against the surfeit of emotions triggered by thoughts of his father.

'Not quite, Your Majesty,' Ali replied, shifting the pen yet again.

Tahir suppressed a sigh. 'What is it, Ali? Has my brother landed himself in the papers again?' His brother, Javid, much to Tahir's constant disgruntlement, was 'living his best life', which inevitably meant dragging Tahir's treasured homeland of Jukrat into the spotlight just for the hell of it. Luckily for him, Javid hadn't done anything scandalously outrageous enough…*yet*…

Infuriatingly, his younger brother had learned to skate close to the line without stepping over it. For now, Tahir had let him be because, when he cast aside his playboy ways long enough to do his duty, Javid was the most astute diplomat Tahir had ever come across. He could saunter into near-crisis international incidents and un-ruffle feathers with jaw-dropping proficiency.

Unfortunately, it was the same brilliant technique his brother used to seduce the clothes off some of the most beautiful and influential women in the world. On a regular, tabloid-salivating basis.

Tahir himself preferred much more discreet liaisons and not just because his spotlight was much brighter as the unmarried ruler of Jukrat, but because of another viciously learned lesson from *that* incident twelve years ago.

Dragging himself away from another unwanted memory jaunt, he fixed a gimlet stare at his aide. 'I don't have all day.'

Ali cleared his throat. 'My apologies, Your Majesty. No, this isn't about your brother. His Royal Highness the Prince is behaving himself.'

'Then what is it? Spit it out, Ali.'

'The palace guards have reported a…visitor who insists on seeing you.'

He frowned, the statement as peculiar as the tone of voice his aide was using. Reluctant. Pained. Almost…trepidatious. 'Correct me if I'm wrong, but isn't there protocol for assessing visitors? Protocol you yourself had a hand in drafting a decade ago?'

'There is, sire.'

Tahir exhaled, impatience growling to be freed. 'Then I fail to see the problem. I fail to see why a random visitor at the palace gates should raise this level of concern with you.'

'The problem is that she's been camped at the gates for three days. And attempts to turn her away aren't working.'

Tahir pinched the bridge of his nose, started to open his mouth to dismiss this subject altogether, then tensed as a dart of *something* speared him. 'She?'

'Yes, Your Majesty. The visitor is a woman.'

Tahir stopped himself from rolling his eyes and stating the obvious. 'There must be some reason you're furnishing me with this information?'

'It's her identity, Your Majesty. I had palace security double-check it this morning after she finally told us who she was.'

That faintest tendril of unease grew into an icy breeze down his back.

He resisted the urge to bunch his fists, instead lacing his fingers on top of his desk, inhaling long and slow. 'Have you known me to enjoy mystery or intrigue, Ali?'

His aide cracked a microscopic wry smile before shaking his head. 'No, Your Majesty.'

'Then I caution you to avoid it now,' he replied tightly.

Ali cleared his throat, moved his pen another fraction, then, 'The visitor is a Miss Lauren Winchester, Your Majesty—'

Tahir jerked upright, sending his chair skidding back on the polished floor.

Suddenly, the vast office felt like an airtight

cage, closing in on him with alarming speed. A glass cage where all his emotions were on display. Shock. Shame. Fury. Despair. Everything he'd suffered during those three harrowing days in England. *When he'd been at her mercy.*

'What did you say?' he demanded, his voice, unlike the turbulence coursing through him, thankfully bled of all emotion except chilling fury.

Now he understood his aide's hesitancy. Just as he fully grasped the term 'shoot the messenger'. Because he was furious with Ali for dropping this forbidden name into his life. For breathing it into existence in this space of measured contemplation and incisive forward-thinking. In this imperial domain where every brave and worthy decision about his kingdom was taken with a level head.

'I'm sorry, sire. We tried to make the problem go away but…'

His eyes narrowed. 'But what?'

Ali shrugged. 'She's been careful to make an appearance at the right times. She knows the protocol well enough not to stray outside the parameters of the law, like some occasional protestors do.'

Of course, she did.

Lauren Winchester had a sharp, brilliant mind.

It was the first thing he'd gleaned about her when he'd strayed into that geo-politics Q&A at his university in England twelve years ago. He'd lingered in the back, watching the woman who faced away from him run rings around some of the most learned professors and gurus in the field.

At first, he'd been intensely fascinated with her argument; with her husky, impassioned voice that spoke truth to power. Then the glorious, waist-length tumble of blonde curls he'd itched to sink his fingers into. The slim, elegant hand that had periodically gesticulated and flipped her hair over her shoulders, giving him brief glimpses of her smooth, elegant neck.

Then, after a thoroughly engrossing hour, she'd risen.

Turned.

He'd seen her face.

And he'd been enraptured...

Three short months later, she'd turned his world upside down.

His father had branded him a disgrace, his mother giving him a wide berth because he'd stopped being useful to her. Friends and family alike had treated him like a pariah. His banishment to the desert had been a welcome reprieve, a place where he could unmask his shock and bitterness without prying eyes alternately judging and pitying him.

That year-long cloistering had cured him of many things. Had forged a new path he'd never looked back from. And if he'd caught traces of disappointment in his father's eyes occasionally before his death, well...that was a stain he'd had no option but to live with.

All because of Lauren Winchester.

Against his will, his gaze strayed to the wide window, despite it not overlooking the palace gates. Security protocol dictated his office be placed in the centre of the vast Moorish castle that was Jukrat Palace. That way he was protected from people like Lauren Winchester and the many fervid subjects who camped at his palace gates, hoping to catch a glimpse of the Sheikh or under the misguided impression they could gain access to him by simply turning up.

Unlike his mother, who'd been carefree and naive enough to make impromptu trips to the palace gates, much to the adulation of her subjects, until a near-assassination attempt had put paid to all that, Tahir's appearances were ruthlessly vetted and strictly scheduled.

Of course, a woman like Lauren Winchester would believe she was above such strictures.

Hadn't she been...once upon a time?

Tahir pivoted away from the question and from the probing gaze of his aide. Every cell in his body vibrated with the unequivocal need to issue the command to turn her away, but when he opened his mouth, entirely different words emerged. 'Did she try to schedule a visit through the usual channels?'

'Not that I've been able to verify,' Ali answered.

Because she knew it was futile or because she believed it was beneath her?

Tahir's lips flattened. 'You could've dealt with

this without my ever learning of it,' he rasped, still half enraged at his aide for dropping this unsavoury subject into his lap. 'What were you hoping to achieve by telling me?'

Ali's eyes widened in alarm and surprise. 'Umm…well… I believe it's prudent to not dismiss the political positioning of this considering her father's role in the British government. It may prove useful in the future.'

Political positioning.

Would that any of that mattered to him regarding Lauren Winchester. The only positioning he'd been interested in during those youth-flushed days at university had been her beneath him, her sinful lips, beautifully greedy hands, and bottle-green eyes encouraging him to lose himself completely and utterly.

And he had.

Much to his deep regret when her true nature had revealed itself.

Political positioning.

He silently sneered at the words, but slowly a different emotion shook free of the miasma, tunnelling through to take centre stage. Reminding him of every vow he'd made to himself twelve years ago.

He glanced once more at Ali, wondering whether there was an argument to be made for not dismissing his words out of hand.

There was a reason Ali was firmly sealed within Tahir's inner circle of trusted aides and advisers.

Often the man wore both hats because he possessed an astuteness many underestimated.

'Is that it?' he prodded. 'Or is your penchant for mental chess hoping this would lead elsewhere?'

Ali delivered another of his rare wry smiles and shrugged. 'Some situations need a definitive check or checkmate. I'm merely facilitating an avenue for closure if it's required.'

Closure.

A fancy term peddled by psychologists for those too weak to put their problems behind them.

But...*had* he moved on? Was this unasked for but perhaps opportune situation what he needed to lay the despicable set of events to rest once and for all so he could pursue another subject his advisors were feverishly interested in—the task of picking a bride, producing heirs and fully securing his place as the ruler of Jukrat?

Tahir jerked to a stop when he realised he was pacing; he'd prowled from his desk to the far side of his impressively large office and now stood in front of his father's portrait.

He met the stern-faced, steely eyes of the previous sovereign of Jukrat, an unforgiving man who'd ruled with an equally unforgiving hand. A man who'd never given quarter, never mind suffering fools gladly, even when that fool was his own first-born son.

Would his father approve of the decision slowly unspooling in Tahir's mind? Or would he see it as another display of the gross error of judgment he'd scathingly condemned him for twelve years ago?

Ali's throat cleared. 'Sire? Do you have instructions for me?'

Closure.

Now the word was seared onto his brain, there was no shaking it free. He hadn't asked for nor desired this particular creature to wander into his lair. But would he be an even bigger fool to let her slip away? To let this wrong go unanswered?

His father might have disparaged him for what Tahir had let happen, but from that time to this, no such slurs had dared crossed the lips of friends or foes alike because he'd lived an exemplary life steeped in a single-minded dedication to duty, shrewd alliances and rigid personal discipline.

Yet somewhere deep within his own psyche the incident chafed, like a burr he'd been unable to root out despite his best efforts.

So...

No, came the bracing answer. He could not let this go unanswered.

'Cancel my remaining appointments. And bring Lauren Winchester to me.'

Tahir wasn't sure what he'd expected in the woman he hadn't seen in a dozen years. Precisely because he'd trained himself never to dwell on Lauren Winchester.

What confronted him ten minutes later, when

the tall, sveltely shaped woman was ushered into his presence, was at once disturbing and curiously even more *charged* than their first meeting.

The first thing he noticed was that she was the worse for wear for having camped outside his palace gates purportedly for days. Her pale peach knee-length dress was smudged with dirt and the dark gold hair she'd once worn in tumbling waves was tamed now, half hidden beneath the white scarf she'd wrapped loosely over her head and shoulders.

The second searingly visceral thing he noticed was that—the first observation notwithstanding—Lauren Winchester hadn't lost an iota of her allure. If anything, she was more stunning.

Features once caught in the final flushes of girlhood had blossomed into true womanhood, her heart-shaped face with more pronounced cheekbones drawing attention to the worldliness and intelligence that sparked in her eyes.

When his focus dropped to her mouth, Tahir had to clench his gut against the impact of its sensual curve. Pale pink lips tinted with the faintest hint of gloss, which might as well have been painted the deepest scarlet for all the punch it packed, for all the memories it fired through him as he lingered there.

But above all those significant changes, it was the final thing that disturbed him the most.

She was…*contained* where once she'd been effervescent, bursting with youthful outrage and unquenchable passion. There was a guardedness about her that he knew instinctively went deeper than the warranted trepidation filming the eyes locked on his.

It was as if the wattage of her illumination had been turned down.

Deliberately? Self-inflicted or by another's hand?

He pursed his lips. What did he care?

He remained motionless, as steely eyed as his father's portrait before him as he watched the woman who'd betrayed him cross the expanse of his official domain, the seat of his power and the space within which he reminded himself daily to be a better man than he'd been twelve years ago.

She stopped at the respectable, reverent distance he knew would've been drilled into her. These days, very few people were granted access, never mind allowed to get within touching distance of His Majesty, the Sheikh of Jukrat. He was the ruler who'd taken the passable province his great-grandfather had painstakingly nurtured, and his grandfather and father had then wielded into a respectable state, so that he, Tahir, could elevate it into a formidable, globally recognised and revered sheikhdom.

To drive home that unassailable fact, Tahir remained behind his desk.

Waited until those eyes that had once hypnotised him with their many mesmerising shades of green travelled up from the priceless Jukrat woven rug on which she stood, to meet his.

Waited until those plump, sinfully curved lips

parted on a short breath. Then, 'Hello, Ta…um… Your Majesty.'

Every muscle in Tahir's body clenched tight, the fire racing through his veins as unwelcome as it was acutely disturbing.

At least one thing hadn't changed.

Her voice still held the husky, melodic texture, like the dark honeyed, far too rich and deceptively potent drink his mother had loved. Like the deep, hypnotic tones of a distant bell he wanted to ignore but found himself anticipating nevertheless, a part of him breathlessly poised for the next toll. And the next.

That involuntary reaction further irritated him, enough to make his fingers press deeper into the rich polished wood of his antique desk. To make him conscious of every exhale in the effort to rid himself, immediately, of the weakening sensation.

When a full minute went by without him responding, because he hadn't invited her to be sociable, she went a shade paler, then forced herself to speak again. 'Thank you so much for seeing me.'

'Don't thank me too quickly, Miss Winchester. I may have brought you here just for the pleasure of telling you to go to hell.' His voice, thankfully, was chilled enough to freeze an impressive swathe of his beloved Jukrat Desert.

Her eyes widened in alarm before they swept away, back to the floor.

In any other woman, Tahir would've taken that

look for awe and reverence, for appreciation of his station and power.

But unless Lauren Winchester had undergone a personality transplant, he knew it was a false, calculated move. Born of subterfuge? Of desperation? Or even again, a deliberate erasure of a fundamental part of who she'd once been?

Why that thought grated something rigid and knotted inside him, Tahir refused to dwell on.

The slick appearance of her tongue, wetting her lips, focused him far too viciously on what it'd felt like to kiss those lips. To plunder until they both groaned with desire.

'I hope you don't.'

'Why?' he bit out, willing his body's rude, primal awakening under control.

'Because I had to come. I had no choice.'

Now *this* he understood. This argument he could dispense with easily. As Sheikh, he lived with a daily balance of choices. 'Of course you did. Good or bad. Wise or foolish. There's always a choice. Presenting yourself at my palace gates was risky. Presenting yourself before me now is stupendously foolish.'

A look flashed through her eyes and his muscles reacted again, this time with memory, as if rousing themselves in recognition of an old friend.

Except this woman wasn't a friend. She was *Delilah*.

She'd carefully cultivated his weakness—an intelligent, fiercely forward-thinking woman with a breathtaking, traffic-stopping body—and used it against him, then tossed him to the lions without a second thought.

'I... I tried emailing. I also tried calling.'

Tahir's lips twisted. 'That is either an outright lie or you were purposefully vague enough not to have been taken seriously by my palace staff.'

He suspected the latter. 'I couldn't say what I wanted...' She paused, took a deep breath, and Tahir willed his gaze not to drop lower to her chest. To the supple breasts he'd once cupped in his hands, those pale pink nipples he'd feasted on like a starving man granted a feast that would sate for a while but never fully satisfy, making him a slave to his lusts. *To her.* 'This matter is private,' she finished.

He ignored the sharp curiosity her response triggered. Curiosity was what had led him down the path to near-destruction twelve years ago.

'Tell me, Miss Winchester, does your Queen invite strangers in who turn up at her front gates demanding to speak to her?'

She flinched at his formal address. Then her lips, *still* sumptuous, *still* far too distracting, pursed. 'Of course not. But like I said, I had no choice.'

'You could've left. Returned to whatever hole you crawled out of.'

She gripped the strap of her handbag until her knuckles turned white, her nostrils quivering as she inhaled slowly. 'I couldn't,' she whispered urgently. 'This is important.'

He ignored the effort it took to stop her words from sneaking beneath his armour. But he managed it...*just*. 'My great-grandfather was assassinated by one of his subjects invited in from the palace gates. Did you know that?'

Her head shot up, eyes widening, her gaze direct and curious. 'What? No, I...didn't. I'm...sorry—'

'Oh, yes. My mother, too, came close to an unfortunate brush with harm by believing all her subjects were benign creatures she could indulge at her whim. She was cuddling a subject's infant when the attempt on her life was made. So you see how pandering to random strangers who turn up at my palace gates is ill-advised?'

She sucked in a quick, affronted breath and swiftly shook her head. 'I'd never... I wouldn't do such a thing! Surely you know that?'

'Do I? What I know is that the last time we were together, you betrayed me and walked away without a backward glance. True or false?'

Her lips were no longer thinned in outrage. They parted as she attempted to suck in a breath. Her face was devoid of colour and her eyes were dark pools of false shock as she stared at him. 'I... I'm... I can explain—'

'True. Or. False?' he demanded; his throat raw with emotions he could barely contain.

Again, she shook her head. Denying him or denying herself? 'I'm sorry.' Hushed words, whispered into the chilled silence of his regal domain.

He took his time strolling to her, needing every nanosecond to grapple his emotions under control. A dozen feet away, he stopped. 'Look at me,' he ordered, every right bestowed on him as the ruler of his prosperous kingdom throbbing in his voice and brooking no disobedience.

Slowly, her head lifted, her lushly fringed eyelashes. Then those green pools were snagging him again, luring him into their endless depths. He resisted. Because he was no longer the clueless fool he'd once been.

And Tahir Al-Jukrat took pleasure in uttering the three simple words. 'Apology *not* accepted.'

Her throat moved in a swallow and for a flash of a second, Tahir mourned the vibrant woman who'd gone toe to toe with him; their intensely stimulating conversations lasting well into the early hours of the morning, when the only thing that'd worn them out further was the marathon sex culminating it.

Despising the heat billowing freely inside him at the memory, he folded his arms and pierced her with another look.

'I understand that you're angry—'

'You do, do you? Or are you merely trotting out platitudes in the hopes that I'll be placated long enough to listen to whatever reason has brought you here? What is it? A bureaucratic favour of some sort? I'm assuming you followed your passion and went into the public sector?'

He prided himself for having never once been tempted enough to look her up. Lauren Winchester had taken far too much real estate in his head during his year-long internment in the desert for him to waste further time on her once his punishment was complete, especially with his father's disappointment branded into his soul. No, his time was better spent pursuing the goal he'd temporarily lost track of—following his forebears' footsteps and cementing the foundations needed to become the sovereign ruler of his beloved kingdom as his destiny dictated.

'Yes, I did…in a way.'

He resisted the urge to ask what she meant, focusing when she spoke again.

'But I'm not here on my own behalf.'

Several turbulent emotions spiralled through him, making him wonder if perhaps he should've reconsidered this meeting. Because he seemed patently ill-equipped to deal with the notion that she hadn't come here to beg his forgiveness. Or even seek an audience with him on her own behalf.

She was here…*for someone else.*

His gaze dropped to her fingers. Her *ringless* fingers. But the observation did nothing to ease his agitation. Lauren Winchester not displaying conventional signs of matrimony didn't mean she hadn't beguiled another unsuspecting fool.

Tahir recalled her family circumstances. A set

of arrogant parents, especially a father whose lofty cabinet minister position he bandied about like a threat. A younger brother who believed the sun rose and set on his good looks and upper-class connections. He'd been frequently stunned at how different Lauren had turned out compared to her family.

Only to discover she'd been better at hiding her true nature…

Now she was here. To seek a favour for a lover? A husband? Someone significant enough to merit a three-day sit-in at his palace gates when he, Tahir, had only received a callous dismissal?

Wrestling the bitter memories back under his iron-willed control, he made the *other* snap decision he should've made when Ali informed him of his visitor's identity. To place this woman firmly back in his past where she belonged.

'You and I have no business together, Miss Winchester. You'll be escorted out of my palace. I strongly recommend you do not return.'

She gasped, her eyes growing wide and imploring as Tahir pressed the intercom to summon Ali. The sound of the doors opening promptly made her take a single, desperate step towards him.

'I beg you to hear me out.'

He directed a grim smile at her. 'I suggest you do not come any closer. My security turns rabid at such behaviour.'

She froze and, somewhere deep within him, he

experienced a sliver of satisfaction that was infuri-atingly snuffed out instantly by disquiet.

And then that emotion too whittled away as her chin rose, scornful fire sparking in her eyes. 'So you truly only brought me here to waste my time?' she sniped.

He shrugged. 'I don't need to explain myself to you, Miss Winchester. I had five minutes to toss away on someone I once knew. Those five minutes are over. As for wasting your time, you were already doing that at my palace gates, were you not?'

She opened her mouth but Ali's appearance at her side and the ever-alert guards just inside the door effectively silenced her.

But those eyes…those expressive, unforgettable green eyes that were alive now she'd decided to shed her trepidation continued to spear daggers into him.

Rousing something to life inside him.

A unique, white-hot blaze she alone had been able to create within him. Tahir had searched for that spark with other women over the years. With each failure, he'd resented its creator and its absence even more.

As he watched her now every cell in his body seemed poised for her next reaction. Waited for her clever tongue to cut him down. Instead, she deflated with whatever weighed her down.

'Please. Ta… Your Majesty.'

Please.

More than her disingenuous *I'm sorry*, this word gave him pause.

Hadn't he promised himself during that interminable year in the desert that one day he would hear her beg for his mercy as she was doing now?

But it wasn't enough. What this woman had put him through, everything he'd lost—respect, integrity, his father's pride in him, the ridicule of his peers, even his mother's fiscal quid pro quo version of affection, something he'd never thought he'd miss until even that was denied him—had been because she'd refused to utter a few, simple, *truthful* words…

'Your Majesty, it is time,' Ali said into the charged silence.

Tahir's gaze shifted to his aide and read the speculation in the older man's eyes. He didn't answer. He stepped away from his desk and, without a word to either of them, strode out of his office.

Tense seconds later, he heard her hesitant footsteps. Then they picked up speed as he lengthened his stride towards his private quarters.

With one simple gesture, Tahir knew he could have her removed. But the cloying need to hear more of that begging, to salve the wound she'd torn open with her presence, stayed his hand.

Ali, clutching his infernal leather-bound file, strode alongside him. 'The helicopter is ready to take you north, Your Majesty,' he murmured.

'Good,' Tahir clipped out.

'Will you be staying the whole two weeks, as previously arranged?' he asked, casting a speaking glance over his shoulder.

Tahir's teeth gritted. 'Nothing has changed.'

'Very good, Your Majesty. In that case, the meetings with the region heads will proceed as scheduled tomorrow. Then in the evening you have…'

Tahir half listened as Ali droned on, his ears maddeningly pricked to the other set of footsteps following him. She would be stopped soon enough.

No one was permitted entry into his private quarters or anywhere in the east wing of his palace without his express permission. And he had no intention of giving it, he reassured himself as he turned down another hallway that led outside to where the royal helicopter waited.

'Wait! You can't… I'm with…him. With His Majesty,' he heard her stutter in a rush as she was predictably detained.

Tahir continued walking, welcoming the blaze of the sun on his skin when he stepped onto the flat stone concourse that abutted the immaculate lawn of his private residence, and willing it to eclipse the blaze and disquiet spiralling within him.

When his pilot gave a brisk salute, Tahir nodded his readiness.

Then, over the rising sound of the rotors, he heard her. 'Please! Your Majesty, wait! I need your help to save my brother!'

And he froze.

Lauren had learned early on in life never to show weakness.

To do so was to open herself up to cruel ridicule.

From her father. From her brother. With her mother looking on and not saying much in her daughter's defence. When a tearful Lauren had demanded to know the reason behind their treatment, her mother had merely shrugged and clipped out, 'Life is tough, Lauren. Learn to grow a thick skin or you'll always be a target.'

She'd been eleven. That was the last time she remembered crying.

Two decades on, with four menacing guards barring her from Tahir Al-Jukrat's fast-receding figure, she was at grave risk of succumbing to tears.

She'd known this trip wouldn't be easy.

Patches of her shoulders and back were raw from sunburn, her throat was parched—her water bottle having dried up hours ago. Her clothes were sticky with sweat and dirt, and her feet throbbed from standing outside the palace gates for three sun-baked days in a row.

The harsh lessons taught by her unforgiving father were what had hardened her spine long enough for her to remain at the gates, to keep making her hourly requests until they'd been heeded.

Until moments ago, when the last of her reserves had been depleted.

Well…that and the obscure threats that had followed her for twelve years. The suspicion that her father knew more than he'd let on about what had happened with Tahir. Wasn't above holding another scandal over her head to make her toe his line.

Watching Tahir stride towards the helicopter in preparation to fly goodness knew where, she'd felt the last whispers of hope drifting away like dandelion seeds blowing in the wind.

Her desperation-soaked voice had stopped him in his tracks.

But that meant nothing. She'd hoped to ease herself into her reason for being in Jukrat. To calmly state her reason for planting herself outside his palace gates, guilefully insisting that they'd be wise not to turn her away because the Sheikh would want to see her, until his guards had had no choice but to relay her request to a higher authority.

All this could mean nothing because Tahir had despised Matt long before he'd come to despise her. Her brother's indolent, entitled attitude to university life in particular, and to life in general, had grated on the intelligent, focused and ruthlessly hardworking Prince Tahir.

Even back then, the dynamic prince who'd taken her breath away from their first meeting had held a set of values and rigid beliefs that'd secretly awed her. Those values had been in direct contrast to Matt's, who'd believed in skating through life on family connections and cronyisms.

In fact, hadn't Tahir condemned her whole family to hell that unforgettable night when the Winchesters had closed ranks against him? When she'd let herself be talked into taking *the only option for the family*?

Self-loathing swelled inside her as she watched tension vibrate in his shoulders, watched the muscles in Tahir's neck stand out as he absorbed what she'd said.

Lauren would've given a limb not to be standing here surrounded by menacing-looking men, at the mercy of the Most Revered Sheikh of Jukrat, as one of his many titles loftily proclaimed him.

But her father's Save-Matt-or-Else had given her little choice, despite all signs pointing to her brother's guilt.

Her family was her cross to bear.

Perhaps it came from being adopted by parents who'd believed they could never have children naturally, only to discover a year after adopting Lauren that their miracle, much-longed-for biological child was on the way. From knowing, deep down in her soul, she'd never felt as if she belonged. She knew it was why, as a child, she'd gone the extra mile to prove she was worthy of the Winchesters' choice when they'd plucked her out of dozens of care-home babies. To gift her an enviably wealthy and comfortable life, with every advantage at her fingertips. Advantage Lauren had been careful not to squander.

She'd repaid their choice by being a dutiful daughter, an exemplary student, even a stellar professional when her father had steered her—that thinly veiled but ever present 'or else' hanging over her head—into giving up the career she'd foreseen for herself.

While she deeply resented the threat, it was for that child who still craved a family—a desire she hadn't quite been able to abandon—that she'd swallowed her trepidation and shame to come here. Face the man she'd wronged.

Eyes glued to his back, terrified he would start walking again, leaving her to the mercy of his guards, she opened her mouth to plead once more.

Without turning, Tahir gave clipped instructions in Arabic to his aide. The older man nodded and approached the pilot, whose gaze swung to Tahir, then sprang out of his seat.

Lauren watched Tahir slide into the pilot's seat, her last shred of hope plummeting to the marble terrace beneath her feet. When the whirring rotors began to spin faster, she blinked back tears. She was mentally preparing telling her parents she'd failed when the aide approached her.

A nod at the bodyguards had them stepping back, but she didn't fool herself into thinking they wouldn't react if she so much as moved a muscle.

Her gaze met the dark eyes of Tahir's aide as he stopped in front of her. 'If you wish to continue this meeting with His Majesty, you should get on the aircraft, Miss Winchester,' he said in a carefully neutral voice.

Her mouth gaped. 'What?'

He tilted his head almost regally towards the chopper. 'I suggest you do so now, before he takes off.'

Lauren's gaze darted to Tahir, who was cycling through his pre-departure procedure, eyes glued to the controls, competent fingers flicking switches. Completely and utterly ignoring her. 'I…where is he going?' she enquired around a desert-dry throat.

The aide regarded her steadily. 'Does it matter?'

Three pertinent, terrifying words.

She swallowed again, desperately suppressing her anxiety as she clung to that last seedling of hope. Clutching her purse tighter, as if it would save her from the unknown, she sucked in a breath and sprinted past the aide.

The evicted pilot stood by the rear door. When she reached him, he stepped aside to let her enter the rear compartment.

Lauren boarded. He slid in beside her and slammed the door shut.

And between one breath and the next, the helicopter was airborne.

CHAPTER TWO

LAUREN COULDN'T SEE Tahir because the compartment was cut off from the cockpit. It was deliberate, she knew. He'd switched places with his pilot because he hadn't wanted to share the space with her.

Lauren tried not to let the knowledge burn or take anything personally. The sole reason she was here was to plead for Matt. Nothing else.

At least she had a sliver of a shot remaining.

The pilot's rigidly neutral look suggested he wouldn't be forthcoming to any questions from her, so she contented herself with staring out of the window.

Yanira, Jukrat's capital city, was spread out in a wondrous splendour of shiny ultra-modern and traditional: spectacular ancient mosques with large golden domes juxtaposed with soaring skyscrapers, and the sparkling, sandy white beaches that bordered the realm to the south.

Nestled snugly between its larger neighbours of Saudi Arabia, UAE, and the Kingdom of Riyaal, the oil-rich Kingdom of Jukrat, while small in geographic size, enjoyed the same opulent status as its compatriots.

Had she been here under different auspices, she

would've taken time to explore; delighted in taking her first holiday for over five years. Escaping her father's stranglehold on every corner of her life and the increasing pressure of fitting into the mould he was determined to push her into alone would've been worth it.

But she couldn't. Somewhere in the city below her, her brother was in dire straits. Despite her father's warning, and despite the fact that she'd never got her younger brother to warm to her, to forge the type of sibling bond she'd yearned for as a child, she couldn't turn her back on Matt.

Her eyes burned, from the long flight from England, lack of sleep and the emotions churning within her. Her last phone call to her parents yesterday hadn't gone well. They'd been disappointed at her lack of progress.

Lauren had felt an unfamiliar sprig of anger. No, that wasn't quite accurate. Lately, offshoots of frustration-laced anger had taken her unawares, the calm poise she'd practised for years around her parents developing hairline fractures.

Certainly, their cavalier assumption that Tahir, the man they'd forced her to shun, would hear her out had knotted fury inside her. Anger she struggled to shake off. Except she had to. She couldn't fail.

The aircraft banked sharply. Her stomach dropped for terrifying seconds before the chopper adjusted. And she saw where they were headed.

Lauren swallowed the apprehension rising once more, her gaze glued to the mesmerising expanse of dark gold sand.

The connotations of their destination didn't let her dwell on one of nature's most beautiful creations.

Tahir was taking her into the desert.

A shiver danced up her spine, bringing with it rising despair.

She wasn't a damsel in distress. Never had been. But the sense of utter helplessness, of being completely at Tahir's mercy, sank into her like a rock in a pond. She had to cling onto the belief that the man she'd known twelve years ago hadn't completely changed.

Despite what you did?

Guilt scythed through her, tightening her fists in her lap, even as she held onto the thin hope that Tahir hadn't turned her away. Yet.

But what if he did?

She pursed her lips. She'd fight that battle if it arrived.

She was affirming that to herself when specks of white dotted the sandy vista. Rapt by the sheer, deadly beauty of the desert, she watched the specks turn into a large sprawl of Bedouin tents, varying in size from small, individual camping-sized ones to some large enough to house several families. Each one had their highest points tipped in the same gold she'd seen in Jukrati mosques and temples.

Brought back down to earth by their landing, she watched a group rush towards the aircraft, hands raised in rapturous greeting of their Sheikh.

On a wild frantic whim, she fished out her phone. Stared in stomach-dropping dread at the no signal icon displayed on the screen.

The sound of the door opening drew her attention to Tahir as he stepped out to greet his people.

Laser-sharp eyes zeroed in on her, dragging up a foreboding shiver.

None of her family or friends knew her exact whereabouts.

She might have boarded his helicopter of her own free will, but in doing so she'd placed herself completely at the mercy of Tahir bin Halim Al-Jukrat.

The man she'd wronged so devastatingly twelve years ago.

Tahir watched her over the heads of his subjects, the thought he'd had en route, that he should've left her on the helipad, slowly morphing into a shrewder plan.

The initial reason he hadn't had her escorted out of his kingdom was because he'd been curious. That note in her voice…

Desperation.

The kind he'd experienced once upon a time. When he'd been in her position. When he'd pleaded for her support.

And she'd turned her back on him.

But that had given way to something else.

The greater need for retribution. He'd thought he resented her being here on someone else's behalf rather than on her own quest for his forgiveness. He despised her even more that that person was her self-absorbed brother.

His lips twisted as he gazed over the endless dunes of Zinabir, his home for the next two weeks. The soaring cream-coloured tents with their gleaming gold turrets he'd flown over should've calmed him.

He'd been looking forward to swimming in the clear lake nestled beneath his favourite mountain at his final destination; to the whispered seduction of the wind weaving through the dunes at dawn.

Instead, he was submerged in the chaotic emotions only this woman evoked in him. But…no matter. She'd handed him the perfect opportunity to settle their past once and for all. Perhaps it was even karmic that it happened here, with the very tools his grandfather had taught him with.

He smiled grimly and took satisfaction in watching her eyes widen. Took satisfaction in watching her pink tongue slick over her bottom lip, that nervous tic dragging heat to his groin.

Oh, yes, Lauren Winchester would definitely rue stepping into his web.

Charged emotion pulsing through him as his plan unfurled, he raised an eyebrow at her, daring her to take up his silent challenge.

She remained in the helicopter, frozen in her seat, not exactly prey because Lauren Winchester, no matter how much she'd changed, would never be a victim. But the look in her eyes said she knew she was at his mercy.

A primitive sort of pleasure wove through him, settling his intentions into his bones with satisfaction he hadn't felt in a long time.

He saw the moment she took note of it.

Her nostrils flared in peril-scenting. Had he been close enough, he suspected he would've seen the pulse fluttering at her throat.

Fight or flight tension held her in its talons. Except flight was no longer an option. By boarding his aircraft and allowing herself to be flown across an arid and unforgiving desert, she'd sealed her fate. And the truth was hitting home. Hard.

As he indulged in the sights and sounds of the familiar, his brain considered just what had brought her here.

Did it even matter? Twelve years of silence, then appearing when she needs something. Just like Mother—

'So, you brought a guest?' The head of the nomadic Zinabir clan and one of his regional advisors enquired, mercifully drawing Tahir from the bitter thought of his mother.

Without removing his gaze from Lauren, he answered, ignoring the curiosity in the older man's words. 'It was an unavoidable situation.'

'And is this *situation* to remain in the aircraft for the duration of your stay or do you wish her relocated?' Faint amusement now laced the old man's words. 'To your quarters, perhaps?'

The knot in Tahir's gut hardened.

Once upon a time, he would've given those very instructions, would've taken pleasure in introducing this woman to this part of his kingdom. He would've relished seeing her interact with his people.

Then when they were sated with food and wine and healthy debate, he would've taken pleasure in seeing her spread out on the priceless Jukrati rug that decorated the foot of his wide divan bed, her eyes wide and her body open and willing as they pleasured one another.

Perhaps thereafter, he would've sought out her thoughts on his way of life and his rule—the ways favoured by his grandfather that blended a modern parliamentary system with regional semi-autonomy that his own father hadn't favoured. Ironically, it was spending time in the desert that had prompted Tahir into returning to that system when he ascended the throne. A way he'd discovered was welcomed and actually worked.

So, perhaps Lauren was to be credited—

No. He halted that train of thought in its tracks, dragged his gaze from her to address his advisor. 'Have her shown to the guest tent and meet me in the council tent.'

'As you wish, My Sheikh.'

Striding away, he headed for one of the larger tents to the north of the oasis.

Lauren Winchester would be dealt with soon enough.

Lauren breathed a sigh of relief an hour later once the cheery women left and she was alone in the tent.

Those wild, curiously excitable minutes earlier when she'd clashed gazes with Tahir still hadn't subsided. On the contrary, with each passing second, she felt as if the invisible sword of Damocles were swinging closer, and not even her usual pragmatism had grounded her.

That gaze had spelled out that he had a plan for her. One that most likely had nothing to do with her own reasons for being here...

From the avid stares and whispered, lyrical Arabic she'd been subjected to, it was clear Tahir hadn't divulged why she was here.

The last thing her parents wanted was for Matt's situation to be made public. Not that it could be kept a secret for ever, she thought bleakly.

She went to the low coffee table where her bag sat. With more hope than expectation, she pulled out her phone and touched the screen.

As expected, the bars were flat, phone signal non-existent. She couldn't get in touch with her parents yet, but she could compose her thoughts and jot down everything that'd happened so far, starting with her arrival in Jukrat. That way the moment she got the service returned, she could set the information wheel in motion.

And while she was at it, she could draft a few speeches for when Matt's predicament became public knowledge.

As communications adviser and special aide to her father, it was what she was good at, after all.

Crossing one of the four exquisitely woven floor rugs, she perched on the edge of the low divan. She was in the middle of composing her thoughts when she sensed his keen scrutiny.

Her head snapped up.

He stood tall and proud; laser-beam eyes fixed squarely on her.

Lauren scrambled upright, more disturbed by being the subject of his regard while sprawled all over the divan than by apprehension of his presence. Especially when they were alone. And the air hummed with emotional undercurrents she didn't really want to examine.

Her gaze darted to the tent opening, and the outline of a guard just beyond the doorway.

'I wasn't aware knocking wasn't a thing in Jukrat.'

She was sure she'd imagined the faintest twitch of his lips when his stern facade hardened a second later. 'Technically there are no doors to the tents. But my presence was announced. You didn't respond,' he stated imperiously.

'So you just let yourself in?'

His nostrils flared the tiniest fraction and his gaze flicked to the sterling silver Moorish tea set and tray of untouched refreshments set on the table on the other side of the tent. 'Hydration in the desert is essential. Disregarding it is foolish. Why have you not eaten or drunk anything?' he growled.

She started to shrug then winced when her sunburnt shoulder chafed beneath the scarf still tangled around her shoulders. 'I didn't have an appetite.'

His gaze dropped to the phone. 'Feeling separation anxiety from your social media?'

Her lips firmed, even though something inside her shrivelled at the confirmation that he'd never believed she hadn't sold him out to the tabloids. 'No. But I would like mobile service…if it's possible.'

'Why?'

'Because there are people waiting to hear from me.'

His gaze grew a touch icier, his body stiffening further. 'Such as?'

She licked her lips, unsure why she felt as if a lot rested on the answer to this particular question. 'My parents? Matt?' The ice receded a little but not enough to make her breathe easier. When he merely continued to watch her, she cleared her throat. 'But now you're here, can we talk?'

'I'd rather not engage with you while the threat of dehydration looms.'

Before she could take proper stock of what he

was doing, he was striding to the antique desk set in one corner of her tent. The bell he picked up rang only twice before a young man entered. He relayed instructions and the servant nodded with a smile and hurried away.

'What was that all about?'

He poured a glass of water, strode back, and held it out to her. 'Drink.'

Her lips pressed tight. 'I'm aware I'm here by your favour but I really wish you wouldn't toss commands at me like I'm a dog,' she snapped.

'We all wish for things we can't have, Miss Winchester. I don't wish for your foolishness in not taking care of yourself properly to inconvenience me. If you pass out from dehydration or heatstroke, it would be most unwelcome. Drink.'

Put like that, and accepting how parched she was, Lauren took the glass from him, extremely careful not to touch him in the process.

As he'd made stingingly clear, there were some things she had choices about. Igniting the spark that had flared to life so effortlessly between them every time they'd so much as breathed the same air twelve years ago wasn't a theory she wanted to test again. Because she suspected the results would be staggering.

Unwilling to meet those mesmeric eyes, she looked around, secretly seeking signs of a woman's presence.

Tahir was purportedly single. But single didn't

mean he wasn't involved with a woman. As her body seemed determined to keep reminding her, he was virile, a pillar of masculinity who could probably satisfy a dozen women without breaking a sweat—

No. She absolutely wasn't going to think about his virility. Or his charisma. Or the way his body had moved within hers with power, pleasure, and mastery once upon a time.

'Is there a reason you're staring into the water instead of drinking it?' he drawled lazily.

She jumped, silently cursing when the liquid sloshed over her fingers. Averting her gaze because she didn't want to see his mockery at her clumsiness, she transferred the glass to her other hand, and started to shake her soaked hand. Only to startle again when firm hands grasped hers, a handkerchief appearing from nowhere.

And as she'd feared, she had her confirmation.

Fireworks shot through her bloodstream, dancing along her nerve endings with gleeful abandon, uncaring that they'd robbed her of breath. Uncaring that she had to grit her teeth to bite back the tiny moan that crowded the back of her throat. That her nipples and very sex had grown tight with a need only he had been able to trigger in her.

Damn him.

He seemed in no hurry to dry her fingers. His gaze was low and hooded, fixated on dragging the rich linen over her knuckles.

'Drink, Lauren.' The order was low. Thick. Implacable.

She lifted the glass and drank. Every last drop. Welcomed the quenching of her thirst and kicked herself for being unable to resist his effect on her. When she was done, he took the glass, his eyes pinned on her as he deliberately trailed his fingers over hers, as blatant at touching her as she'd been careful to do the opposite. His very gaze dared her to object, to protest how much he affected her.

She pressed her lips together, fighting the blaze searing inside her while projecting cool composure.

Lauren wasn't sure who won their battle of wills. But abruptly, he dropped her hand, took her glass and refilled it.

'Slower this time,' he intoned deeply again.

The rumbling-thunder voice sent sensation skittering over her body. She tried to ignore it but, with him standing so close, avoiding Tahir was impossible.

His scent filled her nostrils, reminding her how much she'd loved tracing her fingers over his warm skin, trailing her nose over it to inhale his very essence into her being. Lauren would've happily condemned her younger self for being silly and naive if the thirty-year-old version weren't suddenly struck with the very same yearning. If every molecule in her body weren't straining towards the unholy gleam in his eyes.

To counter that insane urge, she took a gulp of

water, set the glass down and laced her fingers in front of her. It was a composure-harnessing technique she'd found useful lately, when the challenges of maintaining serenity in the face of her father's demands had worn her down. 'Ta— Your Majesty, I'd be grateful if you would let me discuss my matter with you.'

His lips flattened. For an interminable age, he simply stared at her.

Then, pivoting again, he went to the living area and, with the grace of the birds of prey revered in Jukrat, lowered himself onto the seat.

There he sprawled, like the supreme leader he was, his muscled arms thrown wide across the log-shaped cushions, and nudged an imperious chin at her. 'Very well,' he intoned.

Unexpectedly granted her wish, Lauren was temporarily stumped. Because it struck her then that within five minutes her audience with Tahir might be over. She would leave here with his offer to help or without it. Either way, she would…leave. Never see him again.

Why that thought suddenly dried her mouth while shoving a lump into her throat, she shied away from examining. But the answer arrived anyway, and with a force so unstoppable, she struggled to suppress the gasp that ejected from her lungs.

She'd…*missed* him.

Her breath shook out of her, the fingers meshing and tightening as she grappled with the unbearable truth. All these years she'd suppressed memories of him. Mostly out of shame. But also, out of every might-have-been she hadn't allowed herself to savour.

Because she hadn't deserved even that.

'Are you going to speak or am I to decipher your request telepathically?'

Heat crept up her face for staring at him for so long. She averted her gaze, fervently praying she hadn't given away her emotions while she'd gaped at him.

'Matt needs your help.'

Another chill wave swept over his already taut features, but his eyes continued to burn as he stared at her. 'I gathered that. What does the Winchester golden boy need now? A lucrative deal he's unable to land? Or one he's unable to get out of? I recall he was always one to hastily embrace a too-good-to-be-true venture and regret it in the morning? Or is it more personal than that? Has he bedded someone's wife that he shouldn't have?'

Lauren felt every bite of that acid conjecture as if it were aimed at her, not her brother. Although Matt had done each one of those things.

Her brother had been shamelessly spoilt from birth, his position as the treasured child blatantly acknowledged with every transgression excused by parents who couldn't fault their biological child. Lauren had grown up knowing she was a distant second to Matt in every way. Knowledge her brother took pleasure in taunting her with.

She exhaled now, wishing with every bone in her body that she didn't have to say the next words. While knowing she had no choice.

'It's none of that.' It was much, much worse. 'Matt's been arrested here in Jukrat…' She shook her head, unable to finish the shameful sentence.

Slowly he uncoiled from his sprawl, his gaze not once straying from her face as he rearranged himself, his arms braced on his knees. 'Let me get this straight. Your brother is in trouble in my kingdom. And you came here seeking leniency for him. The same brother who treats you like a second-class citizen? The same brother you colluded with to throw me under the bus twelve years ago?'

If her mouth had been dry before, it turned into a desolate desert at each stinging indictment that fell from his lips.

'I'm aware we need to discuss what happened twelve years ago. To clear the air—'

'Are you? How very magnanimous of you,' he stated. 'A whole dozen years too late.' His tone was cold enough to drag shivers over her skin.

Lauren had withstood a lot in her life, not least her father's constant judgment, rancour, and emotional blackmail. She'd somehow found the inner strength to rise above. To hold her chin up and plough forward.

But Tahir's scathing censure, and the knowledge that she deserved the sharp razor's edge of it, was too much to withstand. She lowered her gaze, then shut her eyes. Swallowed.

'I'm sorry,' she murmured. Too weak and far too late. 'For what happened. I know I didn't do enough—'

'You will *not dare* tell me that you had no choice,' he warned through gritted teeth.

She dragged her eyes open, bit back a gasp when she saw that he'd surged up and stood mere feet from her. A pillar of righteous, entirely justified affront with fists clenched, his jaw rock hard as he glared at her.

'I didn't believe I did. Not then.' *And not now*, she added silently.

'No. Have the courage to speak the truth now, Lauren. You itched for the notoriety your brother enjoyed and selfishly brought me along for the ride. And you did so knowing full well you wouldn't suffer the same consequences I would. You knew the potential of disgrace and dishonour for me, for my family, my country and you did it anyway. Am I wrong?'

'Yes, you're wrong. And I… I don't know what to say to make you believe how sorry I am.'

Expecting another scathing put-down, Tahir surprised her by throwing his head back and letting out a bark of laughter.

'In my wildest dreams I didn't think we would find ourselves here, full circle, with the shoe on the other foot,' he said when the laughter died away.

His accent had grown thicker, an indication, she recalled, that his emotions were running close to the surface.

He'd sounded like that when in the throes of passion, a reminder that arrived with far too much heat in her body.

'The irony isn't lost on me,' she whispered.

The gleam in his eyes intensified. 'Good. Then something else that shouldn't be lost on you is exactly how this is going to go.'

She shook her head, taking an involuntary step forward before she could help herself. 'I...we don't have to repeat the mistakes of the past. Please, Tahir... I'll do—' She paused, aware she was straying into unwise territory. But it was too late. He'd scented the weakness in her unfinished statement.

He inhaled sharply, his eyes darkening to molten gold. Slowly he inhaled, his body uncoiling like a majestic creature rising from its aeons-long slumber. In his dark golden robes, with those gleaming eyes and commanding presence, he was almost otherworldly.

Against her will, Lauren was utterly transfixed, unable to move as he prowled even closer. When he reached her, he didn't stop. Instead, he circled her, drawing ever nearer until the scent of spice, earth and man saturated her.

On his second circuit, he stopped behind her. 'Go on. Say it,' he murmured softly in her ear. 'Be brave enough to finish that sentence.'

Shivers coursed through her, the gravity of the situation drying her mouth harder and lodging a stone in her throat. Silently she shook her head.

'Shall I say it for you, then? You can deny it if I'm wrong. "I'll do anything." That's what you meant to say, isn't it?'

Digging deep to find her courage, she lifted her chin, fixed her gaze on the exquisite Moorish cabinet on the other side of the room. 'Maybe it was. But I didn't say it.'

'Why not? Because you *won't* do anything to save Matt and avoid scandal for you and your family? That's what this is ultimately about, isn't it? Are you saying there's a line you won't cross?'

Guilt pummelled her at the deep censure in those words. But in the silence thickening around them, she hardened her resolve. Keeping her gaze forward, because she wasn't quite brave enough to face him yet, she answered, 'We should discuss what happened between us twelve years ago. Maybe if we clear the air—'

She froze as he gave another bark of scornful laughter. 'What is there to say? You invited me to your home for a presumed dinner for two when your parents were away and failed to tell me a *special* kind of party was happening right under our noses. And when reports emerged of Prince Tahir being in the same location a booze-filled sex party was happening, you helped things along by providing pictures of us taken on your phone.'

She spun around then, danger be damned, because she needed to say this while looking into his eyes. Even if those eyes threatened to devour and annihilate her at the same time. 'No, I *didn't* help things along. I denied your involvement with that party.'

His jaw gritted. 'Did you? Because you seemed to be curiously unwilling to give a definitive opinion after the fact on how those pictures got into the papers.'

Because even then, she'd suspected who was behind it. Matt had denied it, of course. And her parents had warned her not to implicate her brother without concrete proof. A warning she'd taken to heart because, even back then, she'd seen how ruthless her father could be when crossed. Fear of making things worse for Tahir—because the phone that held those pictures had gone missing, along with texts they'd sent each other—had held her tongue. While the pictures and texts hadn't been overtly graphic, they'd been intimate. Passionate. Deeply personal.

The sort of thing a prince and future king wouldn't want advertised to the world. The sort of thing that caused scandals when it was.

That threat of the unknown—and the knowledge that her father wasn't above using it and other means to keep her in line—had kept her stifled over the years, much to her distress.

It was partly why she was in Jukrat, pleading for Matt, after all.

'I know you don't believe me, but I don't know how they got hold of those photos.' She sighed, the cloak of defeat threatening again. 'I tried to convince them you weren't involved. Please believe me, Tahir.'

His nostrils flared at her mention of his name. She fully expected him to order her to use his title as she'd been strictly directed by his aide. But for good or ill, she yearned to reach the Tahir she'd known back in those heady university days when she'd felt as if the world were her oyster and he were her unicorn, a fantastical myth somehow come to life and seemingly interested in plain old her.

She'd never understood what he saw in her but, by God, she'd clung to it, treasured every second as if it would be her last. And with a simple error, it had been.

'The Lauren I believed I knew was brave. Bold. Unwavering. She believed in right and wrong.' His eyes narrowed to guillotine-sharp blades.

Except when it came to the murky business of her family. 'I know it sounds naive but… I thought it'd all blow over within days. I didn't know the newspapers would go to those relentless lengths.'

'Oh, but they did. My family lawyers did their job well, but do you realise what those pictures did to my reputation? To my father's reputation? The damage it did to Jukrat in the eyes of the world?'

Lauren felt the blood leave her face as she stared at him. At the time she'd been devastated to discover that Tahir had withdrawn from university following the relentless hounding of the press and the unsavoury things said about him. Moreover, that he'd left without giving her a chance to explain or beg his forgiveness.

And yes, her misjudgement of Matt's activities that night with his friends had been unforgivable, but she'd hoped Tahir would see things from her perspective. That her family's emotional blackmail had been equally unbearable. As usual, they'd believed Matt when he'd pleaded his innocence and Lauren had felt the force of her father's will when he'd pressed her into distancing herself from Tahir and the whole event once the tabloid press had dug their claws into the scandal.

But above all else, the desolation of losing Tahir had made her shut out the world, including tuning out what had happened to him after his departure.

Learning of the true repercussions of the scandal, of what her failure to back Tahir had done to Jukrat's reputation and to the man who'd captivated both her mind and body, had annihilated her.

'I tried to reach out.' She paused, wet her lips. 'A few months after it happened, I tried to contact you.'

His lips twisted in a macabre imitation of a smile. 'Should I tell you where I was? Give you the reason you couldn't reach me?'

She suspected she didn't need to respond. He would give her no quarter in hammering home what damage her actions had caused. So, lips firmed to stop what felt bracingly close to a moan of despair from rising, she watched him exhale long and slow.

'My father was deeply ashamed. He believed I'd let my better instincts be overruled by a woman. He'd taught me better than that, you see. Believed I was above falling prey to feminine beguilement. So when my actions brought disgrace to his rule and this kingdom, I was banished here to the desert for a year.'

This time, the noise escaped her throat, a tiny mournful sound that echoed in the horrible silence trailing his words.

Something kicked hard and true inside her. *Beguilement.*

It was the same thing she'd felt for him, starting with the deep tingling between her shoulders during the environmental symposium. She'd been looking forward to stating her case to so-called world leaders and government officials who overpromised and woefully underdelivered. She'd rehearsed her speech a dozen times and had been confidently ploughing ahead with the debate when she'd felt it.

Felt *him*.

It'd taken every scrape of composure she'd possessed to finish the debate.

Much as it was doing now.

'Here?' She cast a quick glance around her. But

she knew the jaw-dropping dreaminess of Zinabir in general, and Tahir's desert abode in particular, the presence of beautiful women and attendants who waited on him hand and foot, would've meant nothing if this wasn't where he'd wanted to be. If every day, he'd been reminded of *why* he was here. Excluded from those he loved because of the shame and scandal she'd helped cause.

All because she'd selfishly wanted a special moment with him. An intimate dinner for two at her home, believing they would be alone. A moment Matt had spectacularly and callously ruined…

Telling him any of it now would sound like feeble excuses.

Too little too late.

His lips thinned. 'Hmm. It started here, in this tent we're in right now. This desert was my prison for three hundred and sixty-five days. It's almost karmic, isn't it, that you're here now? Do you believe in divine justice, Lauren?' he taunted, his voice eerily even.

She wanted to say no. But then she remembered her time with him. Those months between early summer and autumn twelve years ago had been almost transcendental. As much as she wanted to explain it away, the uniqueness of their time together had been too cosmic to reduce to a set of coincidences and pure chemistry.

He'd been the fiercest comet in her sky, blazing a mesmerising trail before he'd disappeared, leaving her looking up for ever, praying for either the sight of him or another sign to tell her he hadn't been that special. That their time together could be replicated with another man in another place.

But it never had been…

'Does it matter whether I do or not?'

His swarthy shoulders lifted in a suave, throwaway shrug that said he didn't care one way or the other. 'Not particularly. The consequences will be the same.'

Her belly quivered alarmingly. She fought not to let him see how much his response affected her. 'What do you mean by consequences?'

'I mean I'm not the same man I was back then, Miss Winchester. I'm not simply going to permit you to waltz back into my life and let you get away with whatever you wish.'

'You make it sound as if you were a pushover back then. We both know you weren't.' Even then, he'd been a formidable powerhouse and it'd had nothing to do with the constant presence of the two towering bodyguards who'd trailed his movements all over campus. His sharp intelligence, his ability to cut through an argument to the heart of a matter and run masterful mental rings around her in the best possible way had kept her in thrall second only to his breathtaking good looks.

'No.' His gaze conducted a long, searing scrutiny that froze every cubic inch of air in her lungs and raked over her skin like the tines of a tuning fork, rousing every nerve ending to life. 'But I did let myself be distracted by...*base* things far more than was wise.'

'I enthralled you with my body. Is that what you're suggesting?' She'd meant to scoff. And yet the words came out with a traitorous sliver of excitement. Of long-denied yearning.

Yearning he heard, if the sudden gleam in his eyes was an indication.

Before she could exhale, his fingers were laced in her hair, his other hand capturing her waist. He drew her close. And she didn't resist. *Couldn't.* Because from the moment she'd walked into this palace this afternoon, that slumbering yearning had risen to life.

As much as she wanted to deny it, she'd craved this sensation of his body against hers. Of those eyes searing her face, before latching on her lips, the way they'd done countless times. The way that announced in no uncertain terms that he was about to kiss her.

'I'm not *suggesting* anything,' he breathed, his mouth so tantalisingly close that she felt his breath on hers. 'What you did to me was a fact.'

'And you hated every minute of it?' she taunted breathlessly.

One corner of his mouth quirked. 'Fishing for compliments?' Before she could deny it, he rumbled, 'I didn't, but you still proved to be a temptation I should've resisted. I should've shown you then, like now, that it would take more than sex to bring a man like me to my knees.'

'What do you mean…I-like now?'

Before she could cringe at the quivering in her voice, he was slanting his mouth over hers, dominating her senses with a kiss so deep, so hot, it melted her from the inside out.

Dear God. It was everything she'd missed; everything she'd fantasised about in her lonely bed year after year. *Everything.*

His tongue teased and plundered, stroked and suckled, dragging helpless moans from her as her hands latched onto his shoulders. He was warm, vibrant, a pillar of sexy, dogged masculinity she wanted to explore for hours. *Days.*

The hand on her waist moved to her bottom, moulding and squeezing, yanking her closer until the rod of his erection was imprinted against her stomach. Until she was straining even closer, hunger flaying her as she whimpered and succumbed to the decadence of his kiss. Long minutes passed when the only sound in the tent was their feverish exploration.

And then, just as suddenly as he'd taken hold of her, he was setting her away, his movements far too contained as he decisively stepped away from her.

Lauren swayed, still caught in the heady narcotic of his kiss, even as she grasped his wicked intent. 'So, this was supposed to be some sort of lesson?'

When he merely raised an eyebrow, she tilted her

chin, determined not to be cowed. 'Are you trying to convince yourself or me?'

His teeth bared in a devastating smile, one that was all the more lethal for not reaching his eyes. 'I've confirmed everything I need to know.'

'Which is?'

Eyes that weren't as cool as his words lingered on her face. 'That while you're alluring enough, I won't be caught in the same trap again.'

The recrimination, partly directed at himself but mostly aimed at her, finally resurrected a spark of anger. 'If you're suggesting that I did anything to make you...to disrupt your life in any way before that night, you're misremembering, I think. You've always been your own man. We got involved with each other because we both wanted to. I didn't cast any sort of...*spell* on you.'

Again he gave an almost insulting shrug that said her argument carried no weight with him. 'Maybe not. But did you foresee a moment such as this, perhaps? And facilitate easy access to me in case you needed it?'

Her mouth gaped before she could stop herself. 'You cannot be serious!'

'Look at me, Miss Winchester. Do I look in any way amused?'

Staring full on at him was like staring into a raging volcano. Mesmerising and terrifying at the same time. And no, he looked far from amused. 'The idea that I'd cultivated a relationship with you simply for this purpose isn't only preposterous, I'd have to be a cold-hearted bitch to pull that off!'

'And yet here you are. And the idea isn't that far-fetched, is it? Isn't that what you upper-class set are known for? Public-school cronyism so they can all help each other get away with unconscionable deeds?'

She swallowed at the highly clever way he'd drawn circles around her. Again. Tahir had always had a brilliant mind. But he'd never used it against her in earnest or in battle. Until now.

Lauren felt the ground shifting beneath her and struggled to regain her footing. 'I've apologised for my poor judgment. Are you going to forgive me or not?' she demanded, her brazenness secretly stunning her.

His lips twisted. 'Much like most things in this world, forgiveness needs to be earned. Does an eye for an eye sound fair? One three-hundred-and-sixty-five-day sentence in return for another?'

She swallowed. 'You don't mean that.'

He didn't answer immediately. Instead, he clasped his hands behind his back, strode from one end of the vast tent to the other. What she saw of his profile mildly terrified her. Tahir deep in thought was a truly formidable thing. And if those thoughts were devising punitive measures against her?

Her breath caught when he faced her.

Dull embers were rousing to life in the eyes

slowly journeying from the top of her head to the soles of her feet and back up again.

Lauren went hot, then cold. Hot because for a moment her senses had leapt, not recoiled, at the possibility that her punishment would be a repeat of what had just happened. Then cold because she was instantly deeply ashamed of the thought.

The twin sensations lingered, unwilling to be suppressed as he slowly returned to stop before her.

'No. As much as it would please me to hand down such a verdict, we no longer live in barbaric times. And I don't have the time to throw away on such trivial matters. But your task to earn my forgiveness *will* be done another way.'

His proximity worked a different sort of sorcery on her, making her voice tremble when she forced herself to ask, 'How?'

His tawny gaze lingered on her for a few tense seconds before he looked past her. Compelled, Lauren followed his gaze to find him watching the antique clock slowly ticking its way to seven p.m.

'Have your sleeping habits changed?'

Her internal gauge veered wildly towards hot at the question. She opened her mouth to snap that it was none of his business but bit her tongue at the last minute. 'Why are you asking me that?'

'Because if time is of the essence as you insist then you'd much prefer to get this over with as soon as possible, yes?'

She nodded, glad she hadn't told him to go to

hell. 'If you're asking me if I still function on a few hours of sleep every night, then yes, my habits are still the same.' She didn't ask him the same question. Didn't want to know whether his had remained the same too, their perfect synchronicity in that department, as in several others, not something she wanted to dwell on.

Because knowing would make it harder?

She shrugged the question away as he pivoted and strode away from her. Before she could move, he was tugging on a tightly woven golden rope. In the distance, she heard the faint, deep echo of a bell.

Seconds later, the young man from before returned. Tahir spoke to him in swift, lyrical Arabic and had the situation been anything other than it was now, she would've indulged her utter fascination with his mother tongue.

Instead, she stood, palms growing clammy and her heart commencing a slow dread-laced thudding as the man nodded and left again.

Alone again he faced her. 'You'll be served dinner now. At midnight you'll be escorted to my quarters. And we will begin.'

CHAPTER THREE

'*I SUGGEST you get as much sleep as you can. You'll need it.*'

Those were Tahir's final tight-edged words before he departed, taking the life force of the atmosphere with him. Still a little dazed by the electric kiss, she'd barely registered the same trio of women from before returning.

That same soup of dread, puzzlement and excitement stirring in her belly had left no room for resentment or irritation as she was led into the sleeping area of her tent.

The scent of bath salts teased her nostrils and, drawn to the scent, Lauren went towards it. Reaching the screen, she gave a soft gasp.

A deep copper claw-footed bath stood in one corner, partially obscured by the beautifully etched wooden frame.

'Would you like your bath now or after dinner?' the oldest of the three women, who'd introduced herself as Basma, asked. The scent of jasmine and eucalyptus filled the tent. The thought of immersing herself in the water, giving herself a few precious moments to sift through what had happened with

Tahir, had her waving a hand at the water. 'Bath, please, thanks.'

When Lauren refused help with undressing, Basma smiled and stepped away.

The sensation of the warm water unravelling her knotted muscles released a moan before she could stop it. Inhaling deeply, she rested her head against the high, cushioned lip of the bath and let her eyes drift shut.

Since her arrival in Jukrat four days ago, she'd lived in a state of constant stress about her meeting with Tahir.

The last thing she'd expected was that kiss. The proof that time hadn't immunised her against his visceral impact on her. That a simple touch of his body could create such…*need* in her.

It was good, then, wasn't it, that this had all been some sort of experiment for him? She needn't worry about a repeat performance.

Stubbornly ignoring the hollow in her stomach, she loosened the knot holding her waist-length hair and reaching for the sublime-smelling shampoo, washed and conditioned her hair, then fully submerged herself in the water, willing her thoughts to drift to nothing. At least for a few minutes.

The heavenly smells of flat bread and rich, spice-infused sauces finally forced her out of the bath. With impeccable timing, she'd just slipped on a satin robe and finished drying her hair when Basma appeared.

'Come. Sit. Eat.'

Lauren followed her to a low table set up in front of the seating area, holding a large array of dishes that made her mouth water as she drew closer.

The moment Lauren sank into the seat, Basma started ladling out an assortment of dishes.

'You don't need to do that. I can do it myself...' She trailed off as Basma shook her head.

'You're His Majesty's guest. It is our honour to do this for you.'

Lauren bit the inside of her cheek. If they didn't know why she was here, wouldn't she be compounding her sins by blurting out the reason for her presence?

She devoured the lentil and tomato sauce with flatbread, saffron-laced rice and lamb cutlets, then topped it off with sugared dates dipped in honey. Her stomach almost protesting how full she was, a yawn caught her unawares as weariness dug into her limbs.

Within seconds, the trays were cleared away. Basma approached with a garment in her hand.

Lauren hurriedly swallowed a mouthful of sweet tea. 'What's that?'

Basma smiled. 'Something to sleep in.'

'Oh, no, I don't need anything. I have my dress.'

Basma's eyebrows rose, her gaze drifting to the dirt-smeared dress now tossed in a bundle on the floor near the bath.

Lauren bit her lip. She'd already accepted the

tent, the bath and the food. Did she really want to cause offence by refusing one more thing?

Basma silently held out the deep aquamarine nightgown. It was sheer to the point of almost see-through and Lauren fought a blush as she took it.

The neckline was a boat-shaped design, which thankfully left one shoulder free to ease her sun-burnt skin, so she chose not to complain at the di-aphanous nature of the outfit.

Sending a thankful prayer that she wasn't near a full-length mirror to catch an embarrassing glimpse of herself, she hurried to the low bed set on a wooden platform and slid between the cool sheets, certain she was in for a few hours of toss-ing and turning.

But, within minutes of Basma turning off all but one lamp and retreating through the tent flaps, Lauren was fast asleep.

What felt like five minutes later, a gentle hand was nudging her awake.

She blinked, momentarily oblivious to where she was as she mourned the loss of the best sleep she'd had in ages. When it all came crowding back, she jerked upright, her gaze flying to her phone.

She'd forgotten to set her alarm. If she'd missed Tahir's deadline—

She breathed a sigh of relief when she saw it was a quarter to midnight. Still, she was cutting it a little close, which was why she didn't object when Basma held out another garment.

Ten minutes later, Lauren followed Basma out of the tent.

The colour Lauren wore wasn't one she would have chosen for herself. Her professional attire veered towards staid greys or deep beiges in a concerted effort to blend in.

She would've rejected the deep saffron-coloured midriff-baring top and matching flowing skirt, which was just a series of chiffon layers laid symmetrically on top of one another, if the design hadn't left most of her shoulders bare and somewhat alleviated the pain of her burns.

Dark gold fur-lined slippers too were studded with bright red stones that winked when she wriggled her feet. And when she moved, they felt like cool heavenly blankets cocooning her feet.

The light gold stole Basma settled on her shoulders completed the garment and added a modesty to the top that Lauren appreciated.

The large camp was mostly quiet at this time of night, the few solar lamps ringing the outer perimeter illuminating the tops of the larger tents. Against the backdrop of the canopy of stars above and the shadows of distant dunes in the distance, the enchanted feeling nudged a little closer.

Reminding herself that she wasn't here for the magic of the desert, Lauren hurried after a fast-walking Basma towards the largest tent set away from the others.

The two guards stationed on the Moorish-styled entrance barely glanced at them but, again, Lauren was aware of their sharp vigilance as she passed through the small hallway and into a wider receiving area.

Basma murmured to a third guard positioned at the second opening, then, nodding at Lauren, she hurried away.

The guard parted the flap to the tent.

With murmured thanks, she stepped into Tahir's domain just as the antique clock tolled midnight.

She released a strangled breath when she realised the room was empty.

Half of the lamps had been dimmed. The faintest scent of incense whispered through the air, evoking sultriness she didn't want to feel in that moment. But more acute was the absence of Tahir.

She went to the low seat in the sitting area. Sinking onto it, she stroked the weave of the soft camel hair dyed with deep reds and oranges and depicting scenes of nomadic desert life. She was tracing a nervous finger over the surface when she sensed the laser focus of a powerful gaze on her.

Tahir stood framed in one of the many openings concealed as if by magic but was really a clever contraption of screens, thick curtains, and intersecting panels.

For several heartbeats, he simply stared at her.

Then he stepped forward into a pool of lamplight, and her already compromised breathing took a perilous dive. He'd showered or bathed at some point recently too. His jet-black hair looked damp and finger-combed, and, as if toying with her memory, one lock sprang forward to curl over his temple, the sight making her fingers tingle in recollection of smoothing that tendril back once upon a time.

She dragged her gaze away, but it only strayed a few inches to the thick column of his throat, revealed by the black loose-necked tunic and matching trousers that had replaced his traditional garb. On his feet were Arabian slippers too but his were soot-black with no adornment in sight.

From head to toe he resembled a merciless avenging angel, come to exact retribution for the wrong she'd perpetrated on him.

But the scoffing chuckle that should've dispatched such an absurd thought never arrived.

Nerves, she assured herself. Triggered by the unknown.

In her duties as her father's communications aide, she rarely dealt with the unexpected. Every move, countermove and eventuality were parsed to the nth degree, eliminating nasty surprises.

Alongside these nerves, however, there was something else. Something that faintly whispered of...*anticipation*. Excitement of the unknown. A sensation she hadn't experienced in a very long time, buried under the monotony of predictable routine.

Which was…even more unthinkable.

She needed to concentrate on why she was here.

He paused a few feet away and Lauren kicked herself for remaining seated. But then she accepted that, even standing, Tahir Al-Jukrat would always remain a much greater force of nature than she would ever be.

'Did you sleep?' he asked, his deep voice rooting around inside her until it latched onto something vital, stirring it and promising an even more intense rousing.

'Yes. Thank you.'

One corner of his mouth twitched, and she wasn't sure whether it was amusement at her prim tone or mockery.

Dark golden eyes watched for another few seconds, long enough to stretch her nerves much tighter before he turned and strode to the far end of the tent.

He returned with a wide round tray, its contents covered by a black silk cloth.

After setting it down, Tahir dropped into a cushioned seat across from her, reclining on it with mesmerising, captivating grace.

When he cast her a raised-eyebrow look, Lauren cringed inwardly, realising she'd been caught staring. Again.

'What is this?' She indicated the tray.

He didn't lift the cloth, simply reclined deeper into his seat. 'It's a game my grandfather liked to play with me as a child. You and I will play it.'

She frowned. 'What…now?'

'I did warn you that you'll earn the right to be heard out at my discretion and under whatever circumstances I wished, did I not?'

Cold dread slithered through her. 'I can't…you can't balance Matt's troubles on the outcome of a game!'

Again, the twitch of his lips, those cool eyes resting mercilessly on her. 'Haven't you heard? I'm the ruler of this kingdom. I own the very ground you sit on and everything in sight. But I'll give you the choice you claim not to have had twelve years ago. You can play or you can leave.'

'That's no choice at all.'

'On the contrary. You can walk away, squander your chance to make amends for your sins, perhaps even save your brother. Although I won't disagree that it's high time he reaped the consequences of his actions,' he returned with a tight edge to his voice. 'Or you can stay.'

The idea of returning empty-handed left her throat tight and her palms clammy. Even now, after Tahir had established himself as a formidable ruler, those pictures and texts would still cause embarrassment.

But more than that, the thought of walking away

from Tahir…of leaving things still fraught and un-settled between them…

Is that all? Or is it something more? That illicit tingling in your being perhaps? The fact that you haven't felt this alive *for so long? The prospect of reliving that mind-bending kiss?*

She brushed the whispered taunts away. 'I can't leave. My parents will be devastated.'

His eyes hardened. 'Perhaps I should have them brought here, let them confront their wilful blind-ness. Maybe then they'll finally wake up to the true nature of the son they've spoiled his whole life. But I don't care about your parents or your brother. A few hours ago, you were pleading with me to ac-cept your apology. This is what it'll take to make me consider it. Or it is something else?' he taunted.

She frowned. 'What do you mean?'

'Your brother may be one reason for being here, but aren't you here for yourself, too?'

For a wild moment, Lauren wondered if she'd somehow telegraphed those whispered taunts to him. That hot and cold sensation buffeted her again. 'I don't know what you're talking about.'

His eyes narrowed. 'Are you afraid to test the strength of your parents' devotion to discover whether it'll withstand your failure?'

The truth seared its way into the heart of her in-securities. Into the vulnerable place where a huge question mark loomed over the love her parents claimed they felt for her. Because even before the events of that night twelve years ago had given her father leverage over her, it'd always felt as if it was a contingency-based love. The quid pro quo kind that demanded she behave a specific sort of way in order to earn it.

Growing up, she'd been shocked to discover that, while she'd never lacked for material things, most parents, rich or poor, loved *all* their children unconditionally.

Take her best friend, Paige, and her four siblings, for instance. On the rare occasions Lauren's parents had let her visit them, she'd been struck by the overflowing, boisterous love their family shared. They'd fiercely supported and defended each other from harm without asking for anything in return.

That had been Lauren's first inkling that her own relationship with her parents was lacking. The fracture had only widened with time.

Nevertheless, she wasn't ready to admit it to the formidable man searching out her weaknesses. She lifted her chin, her heart thumping loud enough to drown out the immediate sounds outside the tent. 'Tell me what this game is.'

Something gleamed in his eyes, a mixture of triumph and dark anticipation aimed at the heart of her turbulent emotions. 'Are you sure?'

No, I'm not.

But she curled her hands into determined fists. 'The earlier we finish with it, the quicker we can…' She paused, aware she hadn't actually secured anything with Tahir yet. 'Do I have your word that you'll help me?'

His lips twisted, drawing her attention to the stern upper and far too sensual lower. Lips she'd tasted with much fervour mere hours ago. Lips she shouldn't yearn to kiss again…*but did.* 'You're losing your touch, Lauren. You used to be a much better negotiator than this.'

She pursed her own lips, the timbre of his voice and recollection of the intimacies they'd shared threatening her thought processes. 'Do I?'

He shrugged. 'Convince me that you're suitably contrite and you have my word that I'll consider your request.'

Knowing she was treading into dangerous territory by agreeing to rehash that night, that she might skate close to baring all the foolish desires she'd once harboured about him, made her insides quake. But she dragged every ounce of composure together. 'Very well. Let's get on with it.'

Her response should've pleased him. But Lauren sensed it'd done the opposite when leonine eyes narrowed on her, ruthlessly dissecting her as he uncoiled his body, leaned forward to rest his elbows on his knees.

'I've never understood this slavish devotion you have to your family,' he drawled.

Something sharp snagged in her chest but she fought to keep it from showing in her expression.

'If you don't get the bonds of family by now, then I'm afraid you never will.'

The barb hit its mark, hardened his features. 'Perhaps not. But I know they don't deserve it. Perhaps before this is over, I'll understand?'

Lauren would've sworn there was a sliver of longing in the words and in the hand he abruptly reached across the table to trail down her cheek, had it not been for the austere harshness of his features. His body was still as stiff as a marble column. Even his breathing was carefully controlled as his thumb slowly traced over her bottom lip.

Against her better judgment, she swayed towards him again, helpless beneath his touch. And watched as, a smug smile curving his lips as though he was aware he'd set off fireworks through her system, he dropped his hand and sat back.

And without ceremony, whipped off the black silk and tossed it aside.

Dazed, Lauren stared down at what he'd revealed.

Three hourglasses lay sideways, each in their own bed of deep blue velvet housed within a frame of three filigree gold plinths and gold scrollwork base. The glass looked so delicate and exquisite, she tucked her hands into her lap, mildly terrified that even breathing on them would shatter them.

Tahir held no such reservations. He plucked them out and stood each one upright with the fine sand settled at the bottom.

She immediately noted that the measures of sand were different. Why that sent another trail of fireworks through her senses, she refused to contemplate. Instead, she forced her gaze to meet Tahir's. Then went one better and raised an eyebrow. 'Are you going to tell me what this game is about or am I supposed to guess?'

He reached back into each velvet bed, plucking out three black pouches just about the same size as the hourglasses. 'You see that each glass holds a different time span?'

'Yes.'

'Would you like to know the duration?'

Sensing it held meaning, she nodded. 'Yes.'

Tahir tapped the first one. 'This one is forty-five minutes.' He tapped the next. 'Fifteen minutes.' Then the last. 'Two and a half hours.'

'What am I supposed to do with them?'

Again, he dragged out his answer, languidly tugging the pouches over each glass before reaching into the tray. The last item was a smaller tray that sat an inch off the table's surface. Tahir flicked one finger across the smooth surface and the tray slowly spun. Stopping it, he set each hourglass on top, pushed the whole thing towards her then reclined back into his seat, watching the tray until it came to a smooth stop.

'I was a curious child. Much too inquisitive for my own good, I'm told. Definitely too much for my mother to deal with at times so I was dispatched to my grandfather here in Zinabir during the holidays.'

Part of that tale held not so good memories for him, if the trace of bitterness in his tone was an indication. Searching frantically through her own memories, Lauren recalled he'd never willingly volunteered information about his mother. She'd read between the lines and concluded that mother and son hadn't been close. His desert-dry tone lent credence to that assessment.

'I wasn't a fan of routine or rules in general. And since I was used to a quid pro quo arrangement, my grandfather and I compromised with this.' He nudged his square chin at the tray.

'What was the bargain?' she asked, intrigued despite herself.

'He would answer my every question for the duration of the time in the hourglass. And I would do as I was instructed for the rest of the day.'

Something far too jumpy leapt in her chest as her gaze dropped to the shrouded hourglasses. 'Innovative, I guess. What does that have to do with this? And me?'

He arched an eyebrow, his expression so dry she felt it chafe her skin. 'You want me to spell it out?'

She forced a nod. 'Yes. Just so I'm clear on the rules.'

He spread his arms across the tops of the thick cushion, resting his ankle on top of his other knee. Lauren didn't fool herself into thinking he was relaxed. She knew this side of him too well. He was savouring whatever was coming next.

'To begin the game, you will spin the tray and select one hourglass. Whatever time you have will be yours to use as you please. I live in hope that you'll use it for one reason but I'm guessing you'll be using it for another.' It wasn't a question but a statement.

'Reverse psychology? Really?'

He shrugged. 'Prove me wrong,' he breathed, his eyes boring deep into hers. 'Prove that you're not here solely to serve your own interests.'

There was a biting bitterness to those words that dried her mouth.

He wanted his due pound of flesh but she wasn't quite ready. Besides, time was running out for Matt. He was why she was here after all.

'What about the rest of the time?'

'I'll have the same allotted time when yours is up. I have a few questions of my own. You will answer my every question without hesitation.'

She could hardly argue since it was far more than she'd expected.

'So this is like the tale of Scheherazade and the *One Thousand and One Nights* but on steroids?'

Once upon a time, his lips would've twitched at her wry joke, perhaps even prompted one of those deep-throated laughs that made her think she'd won a special prize by drawing such emotion from him.

Tonight, his gaze merely swept down for a con-

templative moment before lifting again to spear
hers in frank appraisal.

'That was a fairy tale which supposedly ended
in lust and happily ever after. Our story won't have
such an ending. It'll end with you convincing me
that you regret your actions, and a possibility that
I'll come to your brother's aid. Or you leaving with
nothing at all.'

So use your time wisely.

Lauren didn't need to hear the words echoing
ominously between them. Her gaze dropped to the
tray, the lingering, unwanted excitement wisely mitigated by trepidation.

She *shouldn't* be excited by this. She dealt in
the practical. The tangible, not the whimsical.
And yet…something about the gauntlet Tahir had
thrown sparked something within her.

Something she'd be wise not to give in to.

So what if she'd thrived on challenges once upon
a time? What did it matter if this Scheherazade-
adjacent task felt like one plucked right out of her
deepest fantasies? Matt's life wasn't a fantasy, and
this time with Tahir was far from a fairy tale.

At the much-needed reminder, she rose from the
seat, tugging the stole firmly around her. 'I'm sure
you'll let me know when you're free to start this
task. Goodnight.' She turned and started for the
door.

'Where do you think you're going?'

She paused, unwilling to admit his deep, rumbling voice triggered another micro tsunami within her. Neutralising her expression, she turned. 'You've explained the rules and I've agreed to play your game. I'm assuming you'll fit me in at some point tomorrow?' She crossed her fingers, hoping he wouldn't spitefully schedule her too late in the day.

'You're mistaken. The game will be over by this time tomorrow.'

She stiffened. 'What do you mean?'

'It means you only have twenty-four hours with me in the desert to earn my consideration. And your time started fifteen minutes ago when you entered my tent.'

Tahir watched shock flit across her face. Every expression that crossed her face was infuriatingly mesmerising. Hours later, he still couldn't believe he'd kissed her. Couldn't believe he'd disparaged himself for his base inclinations only to succumb to the theory seconds later. Hell, even now, he could hardly keep his eyes off those luscious lips.

'What?'

He refocused on their conversation. On the game he'd decided on his helicopter ride over would be the ideal tool for his retribution. 'You're wasting time, Lauren. Sit down.'

Eyes wide with shock and a charged spark he wanted to foolishly explore, she whirled with an innate grace he suspected she wasn't conscious of and drifted back to her seat.

Sinking back onto it with that same riveting poise, she frowned. 'We're doing this now?'

'Weren't you eager to get started only a little while ago?'

'Yes, but—'

Tahir reached forward and spun the tray, watched the shrouded hourglasses whirl before slowing to a stop. For a moment he wondered whether he was tarnishing the memories he'd created with his grandfather by using this tool. Just as his mother did with him, was he lowering himself by sinking into the same soulless transactional quid pro quo with Lauren?

No. It was the most effective means of reaching his goals. Nothing more.

'Choose.'

For an age, her gaze clung to his, her expressions ranging from wariness to defiance to trepidation. Then extending one fine-boned hand, she traced her fingers over the pouch to the left for a moment before, emitting a small breath, tugging it free.

Tahir had played the game often enough to know which one she'd uncovered, and even as sprigs of excitement unfurled in his chest, he muttered coolly, 'You have forty-five minutes.'

He sat back, momentarily regretting letting her go first because he knew the next forty-five minutes would be about her brother, the selfish idiot she seemed to irrationally care about. He tightened his gut against the faint spikes of sensation that reeked far too much of jealousy. 'Proceed.'

She licked her lips, leaving a damp trail on her plump flesh and sending a pulse of lust into his groin. 'Matt was arrested two weeks ago. He…was told he'd have time to organise his defence team but the court has expedited his case.' She paused, sucked in a long breath that drew his unwilling gaze to her chest and the firm breasts pushing against the material of her saffron-coloured top.

He should've instructed that she not be dressed in his favourite colour…

He wrenched himself from that distracting thought and focused, tensing as her words penetrated.

'My judicial system marches to its own drumbeat.' Tahir shrugged. 'Unlike other court systems, Jukrat has attained its level of excellence by being fair but swift,' he said without conceit. It was a system his father had fought hard for; one Tahir had strictly maintained.

Lauren nodded. 'So I've discovered.'

He refused to be affected by the alarm in her response. 'What was your brother charged with?'

Her lush eyelashes swept down, the first indication that she didn't relish the response she had to give. When her lips pursed in a futile effort to buy herself more time, Tahir's skin tightened with premonition. 'Answer me, Lauren.'

'Drug possession,' she finally said, her voice subdued.

The potent dose of poetic justice being delivered held him still for several seconds. He only roused himself out of it when she darted a glance at him.

'Your brother smuggled drugs into my kingdom?' The words felt like ice chips falling from his lips.

Until now, with his thoughts irritatingly fixated on Lauren, he hadn't speculated about the other Winchester's troubles. What he'd done was instruct Ali to make discreet enquiries into Lauren's life. He knew she worked as her father's communications chief—an ironic discovery considering how poorly she'd *communicated* when he'd needed her assistance twelve years ago. He'd also discovered that her aspirations had taken a back seat to her father's ambitions.

And that she was unattached.

Her green eyes widened, probably in reaction to the hard bite of his question. 'You didn't investigate?'

'I recall mentioning I have very little time to spare for that Winchester. Besides, I knew you would enlighten me.'

'Okay. Well, he said he didn't do it.'

'Of course he did.'

Her flinch at his acerbic response produced a twinge of regret he immediately smothered.

'What is his excuse, then? Let me guess. It was

someone else's fault?' The question was laden with heavy scepticism he didn't bother to disguise.

And even though he saw her reluctance to confirm what they both knew was coming next—because it would be as lame now as every excuse Matt Winchester had uttered when cornered—she attempted anyway. 'He was part of a group passing through Jukrat on their way from a business trip. He thinks one of the others planted drugs in his suitcase.'

'Of course he does,' Tahir repeated, wholly unsurprised the man was still scapegoating others. Sensing there was more, he narrowed his eyes. 'And?'

'He tried to reach you, but his access was blocked.'

Tahir allowed himself a bark of bitter laughter. 'Ah. For a moment there I thought he'd chosen to man up and face the consequences of his actions.'

'With respect, this isn't funny.'

His laughter died off, anger igniting in his belly. 'No, it's not. Which begs the question, under what circumstances did you think I'd lift a finger to help your brother?'

A visible tremor went through her at his chilly tone. The same tone he'd used during their last meeting when she'd shown where her true loyalty lay. He needed to keep remembering that. To not allow those alluring eyes to sway him in any way.

At his continued stare, her gaze fell, then darted

to the fine golden sand eagerly building its miniature mountain at the bottom of the hourglass.

'What makes you think I hold any sway over an
independent judicial system?' he pressed when she
remained silent.

'Matt's lawyer seemed to think…that you would
intercede on his behalf. Because Matt was your
friend once upon a time?'

Tahir had only tolerated Winchester because of
his proximity to Lauren. His jaw tightened with
acid regret at how misguided he'd been. 'Remind
me again how that friendship ended, Lauren,' he
invited.

Perhaps it was her name on his lips that darkened
her eyes. Better still, he hoped, it was her deep regret of her treatment of him.

But in that instant, Tahir was glad he'd instigated
this game.

Because he intended to excise a few wounds, lay
haunting ghosts to rest. And after this night, never
think of Lauren Winchester again.

CHAPTER FOUR

'DO WE NEED to go through it all again?' she asked, her gaze fixed on the hourglass.

'Look at me, Lauren,' Tahir demanded. Now he'd said her name, he couldn't seem to stop. Couldn't seem to stop the flashes of memory of when he'd groaned her name when he was deep inside her, her limbs wrapped tight around him as if he were her only anchor to this world.

What he'd felt in those moments...

Tahir jerked forward, physically wresting himself away from those traitorous memories. They'd been a lie. A lethal little game where the unwary paid dearly.

Not dissimilar to the game he was indulging in now. Only this time, he would emerge the victor.

When she finally dragged her gaze up, her expression held equal parts trepidation and irritation. Why that kicked up his pulse another notch, he wasn't going to dwell on. 'Answer me,' he insisted.

'What good will it do to rehash it all over again?' she answered, a whisker of desperation in her voice.

He didn't respond, allowing his silence to speak for him. When her gaze darted to the hourglass again, she expelled a rushed breath.

'You cut him off because of his...lifestyle at uni,' she relayed in a solemn tone.

Tahir shook his head, another wave of bitterness curling through him. 'The whole, explicit truth, Lauren, not the sanitised version you use to keep yourself warm at night.'

She paled and her nostrils fluttered again in that way that would've drawn sympathy and pity from another being had they not known the depths of her duplicity. Then her chin lifted, and she was gathering herself with that depth of poise he'd used to marvel at. 'You disapproved of his drinking and partying. The way he treated others.'

'Others?' he clipped out.

'Fine, you disliked the way he treated *me*. And I know you think I colluded with him that night. But...' She stopped and took another breath, while his gut turned to stone.

'But what?' he pushed. He'd waited far too long for this, had spent *months* in this very desert berating himself for being so gullible, to tolerate her hesitation.

She shook her head, her eyes flashing with green fire. 'This is supposed to be my time, isn't it? Isn't this cheating?'

His gaze dropped to the hourglass. He'd watched those grains often enough to know only a handful of minutes remained. He forced his insides to relax. 'Very well.'

'Like I said, everything happened fast. His trial is already scheduled.'

He should've felt satisfaction at the news, should've steeped himself in well-earned retribution. But the sensation was surprisingly...absent. It took another second to get why. Because in the grand scheme of things, Matt Winchester didn't matter.

The woman who sat before him, however...

Where facts, figures and the pragmatism should've ruled, she'd lured him into casting aside his hardened cynicism, into thinking their connection went beyond the physical.

She was the one who'd made him dabble in that ingredient that was, even as the young Prince he was then, detrimental to a man in his position.

She'd made him...*hope*.

Made him ponder whether relationships like the regimental one with his father and the clinically transactional one with his mother were the exceptions, not the rule. In the end, she'd proved that she was just as self-serving as his mother.

In Tahir's eyes, *that* was her ultimate sin.

'So you would like me to do what? Call the judge and tell him to let a drug trafficker go scot-free?'

She worried the inside of her lip for several seconds before she answered. 'No, of course not, but you could ask that Matt be given a little more time to get his defence sorted properly—'

'No, that is not going to happen,' he interrupted coldly.

The hands folded in her lap twisted once before she stilled the movement. 'Please…'

'Tell me, are your British tabloids still ravenous for the sort of scandal I was embroiled in?'

She gave a reluctant nod and he stopped himself from watching the lamplight dance over her glossy hair. 'Yes.'

'So why would I want to place myself in a position to draw the same unfavourable attention?'

Wide green eyes rose to boldly meet his. 'So you won't help Matt? Is that your final answer?'

He let loose a grim smile. 'Ready to throw in the towel so quickly?'

Her shoulders twitched before straightening and he recalled her grounding rituals before she took on a formidable challenge. How many times had he watched her do her customary twenty-second countdown and her deep breathing before flinging herself headlong into a charged debate, often winning in spectacular fashion?

Somewhere deep within, in a place he wasn't entirely willing to admit existed, he wondered whether that memory was partly why he'd chosen this route to satisfaction.

Her lips parted, ready to speak. He stopped her by holding up his hand, even while anticipatory fire shot through his system. 'Your time is up,' he drawled.

She snatched in a breath, her gaze shifting to the last few settling grains of sand. Her fingers untwisted, surprising him. It was almost as if she was…relieved.

'So what now? You're going to bombard me with your own questions?'

He tugged the coiled rope dangling from the ceiling. Seconds later, two attendants entered. He relayed his request and they exited.

'Now you'll drink tea with me, and we'll see where the conversation takes us. You still drink tea, yes?'

He watched her grapple with wary surprise, her wide eyes blinking before she murmured, 'Yes. But I thought—'

'I know what you thought. And you'll get your wish sooner rather than later.'

'But you feel like toying with me first?'

He shrugged. 'I recall you being partial to well-crafted coaxing. We're barely an hour into this, Lauren. Surely you don't want to be short-changed this early?'

She sucked in another breath, right before heat flowed up her smooth neck and into her face. He allowed himself another smile. 'And you still blush on demand. Interesting. I would've thought you'd be rid of that weakness by now.'

'Blushing isn't a weakness.'

'But it's a lie when it comes to you, isn't it?' he

said with more bite than he'd intended. 'Because it gives one impression while hiding the truth.'

'And what is that truth? That I made a mistake *once* when we knew one another? Is that the sword you're intending to hold over my head while you play your games?'

The astringent memory he thought he'd cemented over fractured, letting loose disappointment. 'The greater sin wasn't how it started, Lauren. It was how you chose to finish it. And I think you know that.'

His words flayed her open with regret and remorse.

He'd aimed a bullseye at the heart of her guilt. And he'd scored. She wanted to ask him whether he was satisfied but she chose silence because she already knew the answer. He wasn't nearly done with her. The pound-of-flesh-taking would be the stretched-out affair he'd alluded to. But while minutes ago she was certain he was hinting at her preferences in bed, his last statement was much more pointed.

Whatever retributive foreplay he'd planned would be extensive. And ruthless.

The attendants' return with their tea was another reason she remained silent. They set out the refreshments and handed her a delicate cup filled with jasmine tea.

Somewhere within the tent, an antique clock gave a faint chime. It would all have been magi-

cal had electric tension not continued to snap between them.

Her gaze flicked to the hourglass and surprise
darted through her.

While their tea was being served, Tahir had
placed the forty-five-minute hourglass in front of
him, ready to go.

Heart in her mouth, she watched him flip it.

Then he sat back, as if he had all the time in the
world. 'Drink your tea,' he drawled, jangling her
nerves further.

She took a sip, unable to stop herself from watching his strong throat move as he too drank his bev-
erage.

In the short silence, Lauren noticed that while the
camp was substantially less busy, it wasn't quiet.
'Does no one sleep in the desert?'

Tahir shrugged. 'Nomadic life is fluid. Besides,
their Sheikh is in residence, accompanied by a mys-
terious guest. That's bound to arouse a little more…
energy.'

A fizz of amusement rose in her. 'Is this a new
thing, referring to yourself in the third person?'

A glint lit in his eyes but before she could fool
herself into imagining she'd amused him, the aus-
terity returned. 'You haven't earned the right to
ask that.'

And just like that, the mood dialled back to
chilly. With hands that had developed a sudden
tremor, she set the delicate cup onto its saucer.

He took his time draining his cup, then poured himself another after an eyebrow cocked in her direction prompted a murmured, 'No, thanks.'

Armed with his second cup, he skewered her with narrowed eyes. 'The last time we had an honest conversation twelve years ago—' his lips twitched when she winced at the qualifier, then he continued '—you already had an internship at the United Nations in Geneva with an in principle offer of a position as a humanitarian in New York thereafter. Unless you were faking the emotion, you were ecstatic about both. But, according to my report, you've been working for your father since graduation. Care to tell me why?' he asked.

Surprise and something equally disconcerting jerked through her. 'You had a report done on me?'

'I have a report done on everyone I spend more than ten minutes with. It's part of my security protocols so don't feel special.'

She sucked in a breath, digging deep to prevent the effect the drastic redirection her life had taken from those halcyon days from showing on her face. 'Things change.'

That infernal eyebrow cocked again. '*Things? Enlighten me,*' he invited, even as his focus sharpened.

Lauren reminded herself that this was what she'd agreed to, what she had to endure to help Matt. Nevertheless, opening one of the many wounds she'd cauterised for the sake of self-preservation wasn't something she relished. 'You weren't the only one who was affected by what happened. I... I fell behind a little in my studies.'

'Why?' he shot back.

She absolutely wasn't going to admit how terribly she'd missed him, how the magnitude of that night had weighed on her so heavily that the joy and enthusiasm she'd taken in her studies had evaporated. How she'd barely been able to get out of bed, never mind make it into lectures, without the glaring reality that she'd had a direct hand in him no longer being at her side, escorting her to class when his crushing coursework allowed.

'Did your conscience haunt you? Guilt has a way of doing that, I understand.'

'Do you intend to keep baiting me or would you like me to answer your question?'

He levelled a cold stare at her, and she took another breath.

'I took some time off, which meant I had to decline the internship offer. That had a knock-on effect on the New York offer. They invited me to reapply the next year.' She paused, memory searing. 'But I didn't.'

'Why not?' he pressed again.

The painful conversation she'd had with the dean replayed in her mind. 'The dean strongly hinted that I wouldn't be successful if I reapplied. Everyone knew about the...scandal and he was reluctant to endorse my application.' She raised her gaze to his. 'I suppose that pleases you?'

'That you wasted your potential because you compromised both yourself and me without a moment's hesitation? No, it doesn't.' His voice was soft and almost doubly lethal for being so.

Looking into his eyes, Lauren was startled by the veracity in them. He really was genuinely displeased by her circumstance. 'I thought you'd gloat about it.'

A single clench of his jaw. 'Which proves how little you know me. Then *and* now.' Before she could react to that, he continued, 'So the dean withdrew his support, but he wasn't the only avenue to achieving your goals. Where was the strong-willed woman who wanted to change the world?'

Reeling under her father's threat to harm you...
The equally esteem-shrivelling discussion with her father unspooled in her head. This one she wasn't ready to spill so she shook her head. 'I chose to start by supporting my father's position.'

The eyes focused on her contained enough scepticism to make a lesser woman fidget. But she'd learned to hone her emotions in public, to hide her discomfort and her desires, to blend into the background until needed.

'Does it really work?'

She frowned. 'Does what work?'

'Lying so effortlessly to yourself?'

'Just because I don't agree with your view of me doesn't mean this isn't what I want.'

The clock chimed again.

Tahir's gaze flitted over her shoulder and the muscles in Lauren's stomach tightened.

He set his cup down. His forty-five minutes had flown by, and Tahir was pushing the hourglasses towards her again. 'Choose,' he said.

Her heart skipped several beats as she reached out and chose the one farthest away from her. Drawing back the cloth, she exhaled noisily when she saw her pick.

'You have fifteen minutes. Turn it when you're ready,' Tahir said.

She didn't hesitate. She told herself she wanted to press on with advocating for Matt but deep down she wanted to sprint away from how lonely and vulnerable she'd felt after he'd left England. Left *her*.

She lifted the delicate hourglass, carefully turned it upside down, her mouth drying as she watched the first grains filter through.

'You say you won't interrupt your judicial process but last year you advocated for two of your subjects to be freed.'

If he was surprised she'd done her homework, he didn't show it. He merely inclined his head.

'Indeed, but that came with conditions I was willing to accommodate. Your brother's misdeeds don't fall under the same purview. Not even close,' he said with a definite snap in his tone.

'How can I convince you to consider it?'

He uncrossed his legs and slowly rose to his feet. Stepping away from the divan, he strolled to one end of the living room, hands clasped behind his back. Lauren tried not to let the slide of muscle beneath his tunic distract her, but it was as difficult as attempting not to marvel at a sleek predator owning his habitat.

'Tell me one thing, Lauren. Did you get involved with me back then because you knew something like this might happen? That somewhere down the line, you'd need a sheikh or a king in your corner to bail you and your family out of some such a predicament?' he demanded without turning to face her, his voice tight with some peculiar emotion. 'And remember if you lie to me, I'll know,' he warned.

Because he wasn't facing her, Lauren squeezed her eyes shut, her heart sinking. The hot, unequivocal *no* she wanted to shout out stalled in her throat. Because hadn't she heard Matt and her parents calculating just such a thing when she'd started seeing Tahir? Hadn't she heard them loftily accommodating her fling with Tahir because they believed it might benefit them at some future date?

At the time, she'd been hurt and horrified enough to confront them. At first, her father had dismissed her protest. Lauren knew now that she should've walked away. Because by exposing how much Tahir meant to her, how unwilling she was to jeopardise her new relationship, she'd played right into their hands.

'I'll take your silence to mean yes, shall I?' he bit out coldly, his shoulders tight.

'I can only tell you that *I* didn't,' she said finally. 'It was never about your position or your connections for me.'

He whirled to face her and the fury in his face shrivelled her insides. In the head-to-toe black he wore, he was a stunningly arresting pillar of affront, like a beautiful tsunami that would devastate once it arrived but was mesmerising to watch unfolding. 'And yet here you are, asking me to save your self-absorbed, selfish brother when all evidence says he needs to be behind bars.'

'No!' She rushed to her feet. 'That can't be your final answer.' *Tell me what I need to do.* The words remained locked in her throat, mild terror at uttering them keeping them wisely hidden.

The fury seemed to drain out of him, a whisper of bewilderment flashing through the gaze that traced her face and lingered on her lips before it neutralised and resettled on the hourglass.

Lauren didn't need to look to know her time had run out.

That they'd circled back to his arena.

'For the next fifteen minutes, I don't want to hear your brother's name,' he said stiffly.

Butterflies beat an urgent tattoo against her belly, the sense of the ground shifting beneath her feet real and disconcerting. 'What do you want to talk about, then? The weather?'

'Hardly.' His gaze dropped to her hand.

She followed his gaze, almost needing visual confirmation that she wasn't fidgeting. This was what he did to her. Made her lose her equilibrium.

'Are you married? Do you have a lover?'

A gasp left her throat. 'That's what you...' She paused, shook her head. 'Didn't your report provide an answer to that question?'

His expression grew more brooding, his jaw clenching for a tick. 'Answer me, Lauren.'

Her chin lifted, a vital need not to cower before him taking root inside her. 'I know you don't think that highly of me, but I wouldn't have kissed you if I was involved with someone else.'

His eyes darkened, his tongue resting betrayingly on his inner lip before he slanted an eyebrow at her.

She exhaled noisily. 'No, I don't have a husband. No lover. No significant other. I prefer my work to...all of that.'

He sauntered towards her, not stopping until only a few feet separated them and the very air around them was charged with snapping electricity. 'Prefer? No one *prefers* the monotony of mindless drudgery over great sex and the stimulation of challenging work. Certainly not the Lauren I remember, who worked hard and played hard. So you'll have to do better to convince me that reducing yourself to this mere...shadow is what you really aspire to.'

'Are you speaking from experience?'

He lowered his head until their cheeks were aligned but not touching. Until his scent filled her nostrils, and she closed her eyes to stop herself from launching herself at him. Begging for him to kiss her again.

'Of course,' he said after an age, then brushed her jaw with his in sizzling contact before retreating.

She was bewildered and not quite ready for his frank admission, and it caught her somewhere raw and unwelcome. Which was ridiculous because she had no right to this man. There was no value in wondering what liaisons he'd had since they parted. Whether, like many men of his ilk, he was contemplating settling down and producing heirs to carry on his legacy.

She'd been lucky enough to cycle through his orbit once upon a time and revel in the brilliance of his rapier-sharp intelligence, astonishing charisma and effortlessly powerful presence he wore like layers of skin. Her actions might have hastened her departure, but Lauren didn't doubt it would've happened anyway.

Men like Tahir Al-Jukrat were destined for the kind of dazzling, meteoric lives mere mortals could only stand back and admire in goggle-eyed awe. They wielded the very power she was here to petition for on behalf of her brother. She needed to remember that.

'Well,' she said briskly. 'That's my choice. I don't need to justify it to you.'

'Justify? Maybe not. But you have a task to complete. And I want that task to be performed by a woman not shrouded in mystery. The true woman buried beneath this stiff and inferior copy.'

That stung. *Hard.* Because damn him, it was *true.* But she didn't plan to take it lying down. 'You want me to bare my soul to you? Well, that's not going to happen.'

He stepped to the side, then proceeded to circle her, drawing ever closer until his intoxicating scent teased her nostrils. 'Nothing so melodramatic. We can start with why you're sacrificing yourself for the sake of your ungrateful family,' he tossed out, so casual it took a fraction of a second longer for the barb to spear her.

'How dare you? You don't know anything about my family.'

'I know enough about your father's previous business dealings to know the route he took to achieve his goals.'

Mild nausea rumbled through her belly. 'What does that mean?'

'It means that your choice to become a humanitarian was admirable but surprising to me because it was at the opposite spectrum of who Charles Winchester is. To be honest, I was astonished to discover you were connected to him at all.'

Lauren bit her lip. She'd never told Tahir she was

adopted, not because she was ashamed of the fact. No, the reason had been deeper than that. She'd been ashamed because she'd always felt…lacking. A puzzle piece that didn't quite fit the perfect picture she'd longed for as a child.

Disclosing that to a guy as entrenched in his beliefs and heritage and steeped in destiny as Tahir was had felt like admitting a deep flaw.

'Or is it more accurate to ask what hold he has on you to make you jump to do his bidding without question?'

Panic joined the nausea, the feeling that he was skating far too close to the truth sending chilling alarm all over her body. 'I'm not sure where you're getting these outlandish ideas from. I love my parents. I'd do anything to not make them suffer the pain of seeing their son in prison. Isn't that enough? You have a brother. Wouldn't you do the same were you in my position?'

'My brother is my diplomatic envoy and the international representative of my kingdom. I'm confident he would move mountains with his bare hands before he let himself be caught in a situation like Winchester's,' he responded scathingly.

'Well, we can't all be flawless like you and your family,' she said, striving to not give away a hint of the jealousy and longing that wove through her at the unwavering certainty in his voice.

But when he faced her again, she caught shadows of bleakness and bitterness in his expression before it was wiped clean. Before she could wonder what had triggered the reaction, he was speaking again.

'Are your parents here in Jukrat? Did they make the journey with you to support their son?'

'Why do I think you already know the answer to that?' she snapped.

His lips twisted. 'So, your role is perpetual whipping post?'

She pivoted to face him as he stepped to move around her once more. 'Why are you so interested in my family dynamic? What bearing does it have on my presence here?'

The twist deepened, drawing her attention to the far too sensual curve of his lower lip. To the firm smoothness of it. To the memory of feeling it pressed in carnal pleasure against hers. 'You were about to tell me who dimmed your light.'

The statement caught her on the raw, making her belly clench against the verbal punch. She raised her chin and tried to brazen it out. 'Don't we all have lofty ideas about who and what we want to be when we're young?' She pulled off a nonchalant shrug.

For the longest time, he simply stared at her. 'Lie to yourself if you must. But don't lie to me,' he said through gritted teeth, his piercing gaze pinning her in place.

Frustration clawing through her, she threw up her arms. 'Why does it matter?'

'Because you pulled the wool over my eyes once.

I don't intend for you to do so again. Tell me the real reason why, Lauren.'

Her breath shook out of her, the sound of her name on his lips snaking familiar sensations through her. She battled past it and gave him the only answer she could. 'My father can't afford any hint of a scandal right now. You probably know he's lobbying for a different cabinet position. He asked me to come, and I agreed. If I seem like a... different person from who you think I was before, it's because I entered the real world and accepted that certain ideals were best left behind.' Ideals her father had warned her off the bat he would oppose once he was in office when he'd announced his intention to seek a cabinet ministerial position six years ago. He'd cautioned her not to embarrass him...*or else*, then coaxed her to join his staff, with a promise of backing her once he left office.

Lauren had had no choice but to place her goals on ice, praying her father would be done with politics in the four years he'd insisted he intended to be minister. But Charles Winchester had tasted true power. And when his party had won re-election, he'd fully embraced that power.

Two years, she silently repeated to herself.

Two more years and she'd be free.

Until then...

She raised her gaze to Tahir's and tried not to be cowed by the penetrating look he levelled on her. 'Your fifteen minutes is also up. Shall I spin again?'

Without waiting for his answer, she returned to the divan. Until that moment, Lauren had believed herself entirely too pragmatic to rely on luck. But then she found herself tucking one hand into her lap out of view of Tahir's mocking eyes, and carefully crossing her fingers.

The other reached out, a slight trembling seizing them as she spun the tiny roulette tray to play the game that was turning out to be far more emotionally draining than she'd anticipated. It was why she wished for the fullest time span of the three.

A relieved gasp broke free when she lifted the silk cloth, and her wish was granted.

Golden sand filled the bottom half almost to the brim and she was tempted to stroke it in gratitude. She didn't because Tahir was joining her, and the tingling in her body was absorbing all of her attention.

He settled himself opposite her, his gaze drifting from her face to the hourglass and back again. 'You seem relieved. But you forget when it ends I have you for two and a half hours too. You barely withstood the last fifteen minutes.'

I have you...

Lauren suppressed the short burst of intense fire that lit through her belly. They didn't mean anything. 'Have at it. I can take whatever you throw at me,' she responded with much more bravery than her quivering insides indicated.

If she'd expected him to be irritated or chilled by

her response, she was to be disappointed. For the first time tonight, Tahir appeared…amused. True, the humour was hard-edged and faintly mocking but—she admitted as her heart lurched—it was both better and worse than what she'd suffered so far.

'Challenge accepted.'

The deeply intoned words burrowed into her, rousing even more memories. Rousing her from the state of inertia and apathy she seemed to have fallen into recently. She might have been looking directly at Tahir but in her periphery, colours and textures suddenly seemed brighter, more vibrant. The way they had when she'd been with him twelve years ago before it'd all turned to ash.

Which meant what…?

God, she was off her rocker!

Pulling herself away from fanciful thoughts, she reached for the hourglass, inhaled to steady herself, and turned it upside down.

CHAPTER FIVE

TAHIR PREPARED HIMSELF for another lengthy plea on behalf of her brother, the distaste in his mouth souring further as anxiety flashed across her face.

For a moment or two in the last fifteen minutes, he'd caught glimpses of the woman he remembered. He despised this new, unflattering, uninspired version—the one brainwashed into believing she wasn't worthy of the aspirations she'd passionately advocated for. It grated that the women-championing, aspiring humanitarian had meekly accepted the role of a glorified secretary.

He frowned inwardly.

Why was it important? He didn't…*shouldn't* care about the altered trajectory of her once promising destiny. And yet…

He shifted in his seat, berating himself to move on.

His gaze dropped to the trickling sand, noting that almost a minute had passed. 'Cat got your tongue?'

She startled, the beginnings of a blush tingeing her cheeks before her gaze darted away. A spark ignited in his groin, triggering another wave of unease. So what if that refreshing reaction still lingered despite the disappointing changes?

He watched her take a long, steady breath, her eyes lingering on the hourglass before rising to his.

'Tell me about your grandfather.'

It took a few stunned seconds for her left-field, soft-spoken request to penetrate. He stiffened, a frown knotting his forehead. 'Excuse me?'

The tiniest hint of a smile appeared; the kind that said she knew she'd surprised him. Wariness gripped him as she watched him, irritatingly patient while she awaited his answer. 'Why?' he gritted out.

She shrugged. 'I have some time.'

He cocked an eyebrow. 'And this is how you wish to spend it?' Surprise was giving way to another emotion, one he didn't want to entertain. *Warmth.*

She couldn't know his grandfather had been his favourite person in the world, that he'd treasured the days of the year he'd spent with him in the desert. More than that, Tahir needed to harden his heart against the possibility that this was a ploy to soften him up, her ultimate goal still very much in play.

His grim smile made her stiffen.

'If I discover that this is a ruse to win me to your desires, know that the punishment will be swift and merciless.'

She paled, all hints of that blush disappearing as her eyes widened with hurt. 'You think I'm asking just to butter you up?'

'Are you not?'

The hurt intensified and pinpricks of guilt burrowed into him.

He had nothing to be guilty of.

Her tongue slicked over her bottom lip and the tension ratcheted up inside him. 'Discussing Matt triggers animosity between us. I… I just thought you…we might both want a break from it.'

'And my feelings matter to you?' he asked drolly.

'Of course they do.' She swallowed and shook her head. 'Believe it or not, while I intend to keep advocating for my brother, I don't want to spend what's left of my twenty-four hours trading barbs with you.'

'Said the woman who once took the floor of a debate tournament for twenty-seven hours straight with only a handful of short breaks.'

She gave a soft gasp. 'You remember that?'

He shrugged, a little annoyed with himself for dredging up that memory. 'I've forgotten very little of my time at university.' He'd meant it to sting and to generalise, but his brain supplied other, more carnal reminders, throwing even wider the funnel of heat attacking his insides. Like how *thoroughly*, *exhaustively* and *passionately* they'd celebrated after she'd won that debate.

Briefly, he wished he'd agreed to Javid's request for his presence this week at the international trade summit in Toronto. It would've been a good opportunity to indulge in a discreet liaison—the type he could no longer enjoy in Jukrat without inviting wild speculation about his future bride—to alleviate the hunger prowling within him. Wished he hadn't broken off the years-long understanding he'd had with a certain female head of state who valued discretion and the need to blow off steam in bed as much as he did.

He suppressed the persistent tug of need and focused as Lauren responded. 'Then you'll know that the quickest way to burnout is to go full pelt right out of the gate?'

Lips thinning, he wanted to condemn her for playing games with him, but hadn't he started this very game? Hadn't he given her the very tool with which she was setting up her own offensive even though she would lose in the end?

Irritated but fractionally impressed by her tactic, he rose and headed for the cabinet tucked discreetly into one corner of his living room.

While alcohol consumption was allowed in Jukrat, it was still a young law, passed by his grandfather a handful of decades ago. More than half of his kingdom still practised a teetotal life, and Tahir respected that by not flaunting his curated alcohol collection.

Throwing the cabinet open, he made his selection and picked up the glasses.

Turning around, he froze.

The sight of her slim torso, of the long braid teasing the small of her back, of the legs she'd tucked beneath her some time in the last few minutes, all reeked far too much of another place. Another time.

He'd been granted the perfect conduit through which to deliver his retribution for what Lauren Winchester had done to him.

And he was serving her wine?

Just then she glanced over her shoulder, her eyes moving from his face to the bottle he clutched before her eyes widened, accurately reflecting the astonishment moving through his own gut.

After several beats, one corner of her mouth twitched but didn't produce a full smile, perhaps when she noticed his stillness. 'Are we moving into the drinking part of the game?' she asked with forced gaiety.

Tahir shrugged. This small misstep needn't derail his intentions. Hell, it might even lull her into a false sense of security. 'You were partial to decent vintage Shiraz if I recall.'

This time her blush flowed higher and deepened, bringing his attention to her high cheekbones and plump lips. Cementing the thought that, yes, he much preferred her this way. A combination of wit, beauty and intelligence.

His fingers tightened on the bottle, the warning that this was veering down a risky path whispering at the back of his head.

'So are we going to drink it or stare at it?'

Tahir caught the nerves in her voice, and he was unapologetic enough to admit that satisfied him.

Nerves would keep her on her toes, dissolve any illusion of sneaking beneath his guard. 'No one else within this kingdom or outside it would dare speak to me this way, do you know that?' he breathed as he returned to the seating area.

Then the reaction he'd expected fully materialised. Her lashes swept down but not before he caught the flash of defiance. 'You said you preferred plain speaking. I'm accommodating you.'

The spark within threatened to turn into a flame, channelling his thoughts towards a different, *beautifully dirty* sort of accommodating.

Yes, he really should've gone to Toronto.

But then you'd have missed her...

'To your earlier comment about trading barbs, I'm far from fragile. I'd have to be made of sterner stuff than that to rule a kingdom.'

The cue did its job of reminding her of his position.

She cast a look around her, taking in the antique furnishings, some of which had belonged to his great-great-grandfather, before returning to him. And why that mildly awed look from those stunning eyes should've fanned the flame of the infernal heat gripping him, he wasn't in the mood to analyse.

'It's…being here in this tent. It almost makes me forget—' She stopped herself but they both knew what she'd meant.

'You'll do well not to,' he cautioned, the gravity in his tone meant as much for him as for her. He couldn't lose sight of what her presence meant. Or of his destiny both within and outside the weathered camel's wool structure that formed his shelter.

She stiffened, then gave a curt nod. 'I won't.' After a moment's pause, she continued. 'So, is discussing your grandfather off the table?'

He debated his answer a fraction longer, uncorked the wine to let it sit while she tried to disguise her uneasiness. Deciding that there was nothing to be lost by divulging general information she could discover within a coffee-table book on Jukrat, he exhaled.

'My grandfather was a great man, the visionary who dragged Jukrat into the twentieth century. It's why you'll find his name plastered on buildings, airports and monuments all over the kingdom.'

Her gaze had returned to him while he spoke and now her pert nose wrinkled. 'I was hoping for more than a sound bite straight from the PR's office.'

Shut her down. Remind her this isn't a social visit.

But his gaze fell on the hourglasses. He'd left the door open by telling her a deeply personal memory, so, really, he had himself to blame.

'He gifted me those on my twenty-first birthday but I left them with him so we could play the game he taught me right up until he passed,' he found himself divulging.

'When did he die?' she asked softly.

'Eight years ago.'

Her green eyes dropped to the trickle of sand, the sight that had in turn triggered anticipation and impatience on many occasions, holding her in similar thrall. 'Why the three different measures?'

'He wanted me to learn the efficacy of quick thinking, of making well-balanced decisions, and when to bide my time.' All three of which seemed in short supply when it came to the woman sitting in front of him.

Her short, neatly manicured fingers trailed down one side of the glass and over the filigree mould, and it felt as if she were touching him.

Again, he asked himself why he'd used such personal means.

Again, he shied away from the answer.

'Have you played it with anyone else?' she asked after a long minute.

His gaze flicked to her face, unease moving through him at her careful composure because he was plagued again by the need to see her real emotions.

'Not in the direct sense,' he replied, swallowing past the curious stone in his throat as he thought of his grandfather.

Her gaze tangled with his again. 'What do you mean?'

He reached for the bottle, more for something to do with his hands than anything else. He poured a glass and passed it to her. When her fingers brushed his, he tightened his gut against the flame that flared low in his belly. Against the need to keep his fingers exactly where they were, experiencing the smoothness of her skin.

Pulling back from temptation he had no intention of succumbing to again, he filled his own glass and took a healthy sip. While the excellent vintage warmed his insides, he contemplated his answer. A pat, throwaway response that gave nothing of himself away, he decided. But even before he spoke he knew he wouldn't dishonour his grandfather's memory that way.

'I only bring the hourglasses with me to the desert. When I'm here, I reprise some of the games I played with my grandfather. It helps me…strategise.'

Very few people would dare disparage the Sheikh of Jukrat to his face. From the glimpses of the old Lauren he'd caught in the last few hours, Tahir knew she was one of those brave souls. So perhaps that breath locked in his diaphragm was in anticipation of a bolder challenge.

But all she did was raise her glass, sip the wine, and nod. As if she wholly understood what amounted to having conversations out loud with a man who was long dead.

'It's an effective way of drilling down to the bare bones of a problem. I do that all the time but with cue cards and the timer on my phone, not exquisite hourglasses like these.'

He narrowed his eyes, drilling through her

words to find hidden meaning or mockery. When he didn't, something unknotted inside him.

'But I'm guessing it's also a way of remaining close to him?' she added.

It was, but he wasn't about to admit how much he missed the old man's counsel. His father had cut him off from all avenues of support to teach him a lesson during his banishment. That missed year with his grandfather hurt the deepest. A year he'd never get back thanks to Lauren.

The abrasive reminder pulled him back from the temptation of finding kinship with the woman who'd betrayed him.

Nearly forty-five minutes had passed. Did she intend to use up all her time discussing everything but her brother?

'Fritter away your time if you must but it won't be on personal questions about me.' He injected enough ice in his tone to make her stiffen.

She blinked and looked away, but not before he caught the flash of hurt. He didn't care. This situation was entirely her own doing.

'Fine.' She cast a furtive gaze about before meeting his. 'I have a copy of Matt's police report. Would you read it and—?'

'No.'

Her nostrils flared with vexation. 'No? Just like that?'

'There's no point. I'm nowhere near convinced helping him is in my best interest.' He didn't feel inclined to add that he'd had Ali acquire the report and read it to him over his satellite phone when Lauren had returned to her tent for dinner. Nothing contained in the document had convinced him Winchester was innocent.

'But—'

'Didn't we agree that the only way to sway me would be for you to make personal amends? Not with official documents or appeals from absent parents. Only you, Lauren.'

Something about her name rolling off his tongue sent another sensual wave through him. Damn, he was really hard up if that was enough to trigger arousal.

He watched her jump up, his jaw gritting when she commenced pacing in his living room. The layers of material forming her skirt swayed with each movement, granting him a view of supple hips and firm buttocks hidden beneath folds of chiffon. He also knew without parting those folds the killer legs currently shrouded from his gaze. Legs that had held him captive as he thrust hard and true inside her.

She pivoted when she reached the rug-covered wall, her movement understated grace and elegance but no less riveting.

His eyes dropped to the fingers curled around the wine glass she held.

Some part of his psyche seemed bent on torturing him because, with clarity that would probably baffle scientists, he recalled those hands greedily reaching for him, her short nails scouring his back as she lost herself in sexual pleasure.

Lauren had been by far the most responsive lover he'd bedded. As much as he wanted to convince himself otherwise, it'd been a vital part of what he'd regretted most about her when he'd walked away.

Because, what…? He'd retained some lofty idea that their involvement would've extended beyond the boundaries of their university lives?

When his entire future had been mapped out since he'd taken his first breath? Back then, a part of him had mocked his belief that things could be different, while another part had been rebelliously hell-bent on finding out for himself. That part still resented her for taking his options away.

In an irregular move, his feelings about that must've shown on his face because she stopped mid-pace, her striking eyes widening. 'W…what are you doing?'

He forced his muscles to relax and raised an eyebrow. 'I thought it was obvious. I'm looking at you. It's hard not to when you're parading in front of me.'

'I'm hardly parading,' she threw back tartly but her tongue darted out to slick over her bottom lip, a nervous, tempting impulse she still retained.

He waved a hand at her. 'Continue. I recall you do your best thinking on your feet. Don't let me stop you.'

The glare she threw at him almost provoked a

smile. 'And I remember you like to bait your opponents before delivering the coup de grâce. Is that what's happening here? Are you *relishing* this?'

'That depends.'

'On what?'

'On if we're discussing foreplay or something else,' he drawled.

Her mouth gaped for several amusing seconds before she snapped it shut. 'You *are* toying with me.'

'Am I?'

'Yes,' she hissed, her chest rising and falling, dragging his attention to the perfect mounds.

'Why would I do that?'

'Because I'm certain the last thing you'll want to be discussing with me is…is *sex*.'

The last word was hushed, and despite her blushing furiously there was a wariness to the word that punched another billow of heat through him. 'You say it like it's a dirty word.' His eyes narrowed. 'Has it become one to you?'

'If you're asking me if I've grown prudish, the answer is no. But there's a time and a place—'

'Like the middle of the night, over a glass of wine when certain subjects are off the table?' he finished drolly. 'It seems like the perfect time to discuss why there's no man in your life. Your name and position alone should have them lining up around the proverbial block,' he said, gut clenched against the acrid sensation that felt a lot like jealousy.

'You're wrong. Besides, I wouldn't want a man who was attracted to me simply because of my surname. Is that how you pick your lovers?'

'We're not talking about me, Lauren.'

Her fingers tightened momentarily around the glass as she turned away. Then he caught her wince as her stole slipped off her shoulder.

'What's that?' The question ejected out of him.

She frowned. Then followed his gaze to the distinct redness on her shoulder. 'Oh, I got a little sunburn.'

He didn't realise he'd jerked to his feet until he was moving towards her. When he saw the extent of the burn a wave of fury rolled through his gut... 'Were you given anything for it?'

She shook her head. 'It's nothing.'

His jaw gritted. 'It's not nothing. And you shouldn't keep it covered.' Reaching for the wrap, he tugged it away and flung it on a nearby seat.

Whirling, he strode out of the living room, along a series of hallways to his bedroom. Retrieving what he needed, he returned.

'Come here,' he said.

She remained where she stood. 'Stop ordering me about.'

'Come here, Lauren, or I'll confine you indoors for the remainder of the time while I get on with my day.'

She took her time to weigh his words while the concern-laced fury swirled in his belly. Fortunately, she realised it wasn't a bluff. With far too arresting movements, she glided back to the divan.

With the wrap out of the way, he couldn't stop himself from taking in her slim torso, the proud protrusion of her breasts, her trim waist and where her hips started to flare.

Whatever else had happened to her, Lauren Winchester hadn't lost an ounce of her allure. That confirmation fired straight to his shaft, swelling it with breath-stealing swiftness.

Begrudgingly thankful his tunic masked his reaction to her, he waited for her to sit, then crouched beside her. And immediately realised he'd compounded his situation when the sublime scent of jasmine, eucalyptus and woman filled his senses. He reached blindly for the tub while attempting not to greedily breathe her in.

'What is it?'

For a charged moment he thought she was addressing his state, but a glance saw hers moving from the container to his face. 'It's an organic balm prepared by the Zinabir women. I believe the base ingredient is aloe.'

She reached up and dragged her plait over one shoulder, her fingers gathering any stray strands away from the exposed skin. 'It smells amazing,' she murmured.

She smelled amazing. Intoxicating.

So much so he wanted to dip his nose into the smooth curve of her shoulder, inhale long and deep.

Trail his tongue over that same path, feel goose-bumps prickle to life against his lips.

Instead, he tossed the lid on the table, dug his fingers into the balm and applied it onto her red-dened skin. Any attempt to be clinical and detached failed immediately, her silky-smooth skin dragging him back yet again to a time when he'd had free rein to touch and stroke, taste and devour. A time when every inch of her body had been his much-relished playground.

A soft moan escaped her, and his teeth gritted harder, the sound punching through every barrier and resistance to gleefully fuel the inferno raging within.

'That feels so good,' she said huskily.

'Hmm,' was all he managed, his gaze fixated on the skin he caressed. Once he'd treated the reddened area twice, he exhaled. 'Now the other.' His voice was thicker, hoarser than he wished as he waited for her to present him with the other affected shoulder.

Tahir congratulated himself on keeping a tight leash on the groan that threatened to rip free as he tended to her. But he couldn't quite stop his fingers from drifting over the delicate shell of her ear and the spot beneath, confirming his thought when she shivered wildly.

'You're still sensitive here,' he croaked before he could catch his words.

Stunning eyes dark with lust met his. For tight seconds, they were locked in desire's maelstrom.

Her nostrils quivered and the tiniest sound rippled from between her lips.

'I thought you weren't going to succumb to my charms ever again?' she taunted on a breathless whisper, even as her eyes devoured his mouth.

Effectively called out, he felt the lash of shame, but even more disconcerting was the urge to reverse his edict. To keep stroking that sublime skin, coax more delightful sounds from that beautiful throat.

Tight-jawed, he closed the lid to the tub with more force than needed, tossed it away and placed several necessary feet between them. 'That should give you some relief,' he said tightly.

She continued to watch him for a spell, then, her composure annoyingly restored, she murmured, 'Thank you.' A hint of a nervous smile curved her lips as her gaze glanced off his. 'It feels better already. You're right. It wasn't nothing. I don't know why I said what I did when you—'

His waved hand silenced her. 'You know why. You're just afraid to address it. But no more.'

Her head jerked up, surprise colliding with the beginnings of wary annoyance. 'Excuse me?'

'Wrong again. No more excuses.'

Her lips parted, no doubt to offer a scathing rebuttal, but the appearance of his young attendant hovering near the entrance stopped her. The message delivered had Tahir frowning, then feeling a touch relieved.

He glanced at the hourglass to see there were

minutes left. 'Your time is almost up. I'm told my brother wishes to speak to me, so you get a little leeway while I take his call. We'll pick this up again when I return.'

Lauren watched him stride out, all broad shoulders and immutable power, with her mouth agape.

What the hell had just happened?

She didn't regret not pressing her claim about Matt. The strategy to bide her time was one she knew well. Sometimes the best way to create forward momentum was to first take a step back.

But the last thing she'd expected was for Tahir to spin even more circles around her.

Why was she surprised though? Hadn't he been the toughest, most astute strategist she'd ever come across?

Exhaling to alleviate the stress cramping her muscles, she told herself she was relieved he'd gone, but it was a lie.

As shameful as it was to admit, she'd never felt more alive than when he'd challenged her or irritated her with his insistence that she was a shadow of her former self.

As if she didn't know that. As if she didn't look at herself in the mirror each morning and drop her gaze in regret.

Eyeing the hourglass, she shook her head at the faint hollow in her stomach. Her intentions had backfired. She'd wasted two and a half hours in the process.

But beside that unnervingly bleak sensation coursing through her was a more dangerous one. She twisted her head to stare at the sheen on her left shoulder, the aloe working its magic, and suppressed another moan as she relived the last few minutes.

Tahir's touch had been electrifying, not diluted one iota by their butting heads—cerebrally or carnally. It was bad enough that she'd let out that moan. Worst still, she'd wanted him to keep going, to pick up her taunt and act on it. Tug her into his arms and kiss her again. *She'd craved it.*

She rose and retrieved her wrap and half-finished wine, ignoring the voice mocking her for shutting the door after the horse had bolted.

She paced, hoping the movement would clear her head. But it was no use. The heat in her pelvis continued to grow, sexual need building until she gave a frustrated groan.

For years she'd easily blocked out interest from the opposite sex.

Sure, she'd gone on a few dates, had even had a brief relationship with one or two men who'd sparked her interest for more than a few weeks. But inevitably, things had turned lukewarm and then fizzled out entirely.

Now she wished she hadn't called time on dating when she'd turned thirty. Maybe if she'd taken care of her sexual needs, she wouldn't be feeling this wound up by a simple, impersonal touch from Tahir.

But had it been impersonal?

Wasn't the fever rampaging through her that much hotter because she suspected he'd been affected by touching her too?

So what?

The Tahir she remembered had been a full-blooded male with a healthy interest in the opposite sex. An interest returned a hundred-fold. One minute in his presence had confirmed he'd grown into his masculinity, a powerful sexual being who only needed to lift a finger to have women crawling all over him.

She was nothing special to him. Especially after inadvertently embroiling him in scandal.

Renewed guilt doused the fever in her blood. She was contemplating how best to recommence her reason for being here when the young attendant returned.

'His Majesty would like you to join him,' he said.

'I…where is he?'

'Nearby,' he replied.

'Wait,' she said when he turned away. 'Is there a phone I can use? I need to make a call.'

He shook his head. 'There is no mobile service in the desert.'

Lauren pursed her lip against pressing further.

Surely if Tahir was speaking to his brother, then he had a means of communication?

Suspecting the servant's response was a tailored one, she refrained from pressing. 'Okay. Thank you.'

It was still dark outside, but the camp was slowly rousing, the sounds of pots and pans and strong coffee filling the air.

A quick calculation summed up that she'd, surprisingly, been in Tahir's tent for over six hours. It'd felt like minutes!

They walked past the tents and up a small hill. While she couldn't immediately see it clearly, Lauren could just about make out the outline of the mountain she'd seen from the helicopter looming in the distance.

And like the mountain, at first, she didn't see Tahir but her senses screamed that he was close. Halfway up the hill, she saw him, a towering figure framed against the dark sky. A shiver coursed through her, even as she berated herself for being melodramatic.

When she reached him, he didn't turn to greet her. What she saw of his face was fierce, deeply contemplative. Intuition hinted that it had nothing to do with the words he'd thrown at her before leaving the tent.

This was about something else.

'Is everything okay?' she ventured after a full minute had passed in silence.

His lips tightened. 'There's a situation brewing in Riyaal,' he said. 'It may be nothing or it could develop into something if Javid and my trade minister aren't successful in handling it.'

Javid was his younger brother, she recalled. The irreverent playboy Prince, known as much for his ability to charm women out of their underwear as for his exceptional skill in diplomacy. Lauren had wondered how that didn't create a huge conflict of interest every time she'd skimmed his hedonistic exploits in social media. 'Was that what the call was about?'

Tawny eyes swung to her, his eyes narrowing. 'Why, Lauren, you sound as if you care.'

The barb hit its mark, making her wince deep inside, but she was damned if she would give him the satisfaction. 'You sent for me. I'm here. You can pretend that I do care, see where that gets you.'

A gleam burned in his eyes. Under different circumstances, she would've termed it admiration, perhaps even respect. But it was gone an instant later, the austere expression back in place.

Turning away, he presented her with his profile once more, his gaze on the horizon. 'Perhaps, but for the next few moments, I wish to pass the time another way.'

She cursed herself for the way her pulse leapt. 'How?' she asked, thankful her voice wasn't as foolishly excitable. 'What's happening?'

He didn't answer, merely nudged his chiselled chin at the view.

Lauren followed his gaze and saw nothing but a dark grey landscape. About to ask what she was meant to be looking at, she swallowed her words when he raised a hand. The movement wasn't the imperious gesture she'd been subjected to a few times since her arrival. It was a…gentler motion, an anticipatory one that urged patience.

She redirected her focus to the inky landscape.

Then gave a soft gasp when the thinnest slash of orange broke through the grey. As she watched, the line continued to stretch horizontally across the bottom of the sky, a living painting come to life right before their eyes.

All around them, the desert held its breath in awe of nature's splendour.

Utterly mesmerised, Lauren barely saw Tahir lower his hand, but she didn't need to look at him to know he was equally riveted, perhaps even more so because the ground on which he stood was in his blood, his connection to land and sky and sand absolute.

Slowly, the sliver became a streak, then a forceful kaleidoscope of colour until the yellow took control, the sun's rays stretching fingers of benediction over the earth.

Sand dunes slowly took majestic form, undulating to life for countless miles as the new day burst into being.

'My God,' she breathed, humbled and alarmed in equal measure because Tahir had shared this with her.

Something moved within her, dangerously skimming far too close to vulnerable parts that needed to be kept barricaded.

He could've left her in the tent, and she would've been none the wiser.

Instead, he'd...

She turned to find him staring at her with an intensity that almost made her stumble back in shock.

Heat. Fury. Contemplation. Censure. *Desire.*

They all blazed in a furious mix, much like that kaleidoscope before the sun burst through just now. Lauren swallowed. She tried to tell herself it was the trick of the light, but the lie barely formed before it crumbled beneath the force of his stare.

Aware that some of those emotions might be reflected on her face, she averted her gaze. But like a sick compulsion, her eyes reconnected with his seconds later. 'Thank you for showing it to me. It's beautiful. But...why?'

For several heartbeats he didn't speak. Then his regal head turned, his eyes piercing her with a gimlet stare. 'Because it's worth sharing with friend *or* foe. The former because my kingdom is beautiful, and they'll appreciate it. The latter because they'll appreciate that my heart, my duty and my destiny is tied to this land, and I'll do anything to defend it.'

She was still processing the weighty response

when his teeth bared in a smile that was at once breathtakingly beautiful and nape-tingling in its warning.

'Very soon you'll need to decide which one you are, Lauren.'

Her snatched-in breath stayed locked in her throat as he strode away from her, a tall, magnificent figure who commanded attention and received it, every tribesman, woman and child pausing as he approached.

Many exchanged smiling greetings and received one in return, but his stride barely broke as he headed for his tent.

Once he'd disappeared and she could breathe again, Lauren returned her gaze to the sunrise, now a gorgeous landscape of yellow, gold, brown and blue.

Friend or foe.

She knew which one she wanted to be. But was beginning to fear that, whatever she did, Tahir would always regard her as an enemy.

That insight took some getting used to, keeping her on the hill several minutes more until the reminder that she had a task to perform regardless of her own personal feelings sent her back down to the camp.

She entered Tahir's tent and drew to a stop. Attendants were packing his belongings, some monogrammed cases already stacked beside the entrance.

'You're leaving? I… We had an agreement!' As

much as she wanted to attribute the hollow sensation inside her to Matt's predicament, she knew it was for her. She wasn't ready to be done with him. Wasn't ready to leave Tahir. The truth shook through her as his lips twisted in a sardonic smile.

'How quickly you doubt me.'

She frowned. 'Doubt you? Your things are being packed. I…if I'm wrong and you're not leaving, then tell me what's happening.'

His eyes glinted at her firm insistence. Lauren caught the attendants' shocked looks at her addressing their Sheikh with such bolshiness but she didn't cower or apologise. They *did* have an agreement.

'Zinabir was only meant to be a pit stop. It's customary for me to spend one night with my people here before I move on.'

'Move on where?' And did that include her or—?

'My final destination is further north. And before you throw even more of that indignation my way, yes, Lauren, you're coming with me.'

CHAPTER SIX

AFTER A LAVISH BREAKFAST of honeyed dates, roasted oats in natural yoghurt and strong, aromatic coffee that did its job of caffeinating her, they prepared to leave.

With nothing to pack besides her freshly laundered dress currently folded into the handbag slung over her shoulder, Lauren was ready in minutes.

What she wasn't ready for was the huge camel eyeing her with dark caramel eyes as it chewed on freshly cut grass.

She'd seen Tahir's belongings being loaded onto two four-by-fours and watched in stunned surprise as half his bodyguards drove away with them. The remaining four were now seated on their own beasts, and Lauren felt as if everyone in the camp was watching her.

Even curled up on the ground, the creature looked hugely intimidating and deeply bored all at once. 'Care to tell me why we're not in the SUV with your other guards?' she asked Tahir, who stood imposingly a few feet away having just finished conversing with the camp's leader.

'It's very simple, Lauren. My kingdom, my rules,' he stated with such simple but implacable authority, it resonated deep in her bones. 'But if you're feeling unduly inconvenienced just say the word and I'll have you flown back to the capital.'

She bit her lip, eyeing the creature that looked even larger up close. 'I'm… I only hesitate because I've never ridden a camel before. I… I've heard they bite.'

'Only if they don't trust their rider. Show her you're trustworthy and you won't have a problem.'

'Her?' she repeated tentatively, a little less nervous at the thought of riding a female camel.

'Don't let her gender fool you. The females are often the feistiest.'

She'd taken a tentative step towards the animal who was eyeing her steadily when she felt Tahir's presence behind her.

Strong hands wrapped around her waist, and she was drawn back against a hard, solid chest. Warmth flowed over her skin, suffusing her in heat she wanted to stay in for ever.

'Are you ready?' he murmured in her ear, his breath causing another shiver to steal through her.

'As I'll ever be.'

Was it her imagination or did he give a very faint chuckle? She didn't dare turn to investigate because she risked him seeing what his proximity did to her. How every atom of her jumped in excitement and strained towards him.

Without warning, he hoisted her up and into the

saddle. Suppressing a yelp, she clutched the pommel and fought not to slide right off.

'Lower your centre of gravity, tighten your legs and move with her. She'll do the rest.'

'Just like that?'

His eyes locked with hers, a sombre look drifting through the tawny depths before they hardened. 'Sometimes the simplest solution is to let go and let be. And sometimes it is not.'

Her nape tingled, certain his response was aimed at far more than riding a camel, drenching her like a rogue wave.

She swallowed as his gaze stayed on her for a fraction too long. Then, freed from it, she watched him swing effortlessly into his own saddle, his innate grace and absolute masculinity almost too overwhelming to witness.

A click of his tongue and murmured words and both his camel and hers moved, their smooth undulating gaits settling into a pleasant rhythm once she got used to it.

When the well-wishing cries of the desert tribe faded away, they settled into a semi-charged silence. They were fully immersed in his two-and-a-half-hour time slot, and she was reluctant to raise any subject that might trigger more of his probing questions.

'How will we know when your time is up?' She couldn't immediately see the hourglasses or the case they'd come in.

His gaze slid from the horizon to her, one eyebrow arched in mocking contemplation. 'Feeling anxious?'

She shrugged. 'As you said, rules are rules.'

'I'll let you know when it's your time. Unless you doubt my honour?' he finished with a bite that lanced through her.

'No, I don't doubt you.' And she didn't.

Something shifted in his eyes. She wanted to tell herself that her words had touched him, but his lashes veiled his expression, his profile veering from her a second later, stopping her from verifying that thought.

And because she couldn't let it go, because some vital place inside her seemed hell-bent on satisfying that peculiar curiosity, she continued. 'Your people love you.'

His gaze snapped back to her, his brooding eyes narrowed. Searching. Assessing.

He'd warned her against playing him. Against attempting to soften him up for her own and for Matt's advantage. It stood to reason he would be sceptical of her unsanctioned observation.

'It's true,' she pressed on steadily. 'I've only been in Jukrat a handful of days, but I've heard the way they talk about you, the way they respect your rule. I'm not trying to kiss your ass. It's just an honest observation. You have a lot to be proud of.'

'They didn't always feel that way,' he offered

after a handful of minutes had passed when she'd thought he would ignore her.

She waited for the hard look in his eyes to soften. For his clenched jaw to ease. Because she suspected that she was culpable for it.

'I didn't always live up to my father's expectations.'

Guilt was a living flame searing her insides. 'Because of what happened?'

His lips thinned but then, surprisingly, he shook his head. 'That was the straw that broke the camel's back, as it were.' He glanced down briefly at his camel, his mouth twitching when the creature turned its head to fix him with a censorious gaze. He clicked his tongue and the animal faced forward again.

'He was a hard taskmaster, probably because he had large shoes to fill after my grandfather's rule and felt he needed to be overly stringent with me. I lived with the threat of letting him down from infancy until he passed.' There was an uncommon bleakness to his tone that sent a wave of sympathy through her.

She lived with that threat every day too, but she wasn't a powerful ruler, much adored by her kingdom. 'But…you're accomplished in many ways. Even twelve years ago you were more or less the person you are now.'

He slanted her another assessing look. 'You don't

think I faked it till I made it?' he asked, thick sardonicism in his tone.

'No,' she answered truthfully. 'I believe you'd boil yourself in hot oil before you faked a single thing.'

He stiffened in his saddle, but a glimmer appeared in his eyes, his chest moving as he sharply exhaled.

'How well you think you know me,' he murmured, again after a handful of minutes, his words infused with charged emotions.

'Am I wrong?' she asked, despite sternly berating herself for her runaway tongue.

'No. I abhor subterfuge of any kind,' he confirmed, implacable power in his tone.

She swallowed. She considered laying it all bare, telling him why she was caught between a rock and a hard place, but wasn't it twelve years too late? Pushing the disquieting thought away, she refocused on their discussion.

'So your life was an endless series of hoop-jumping, but surely there was some sort of balance?'

He sent her a droll look. 'You're wondering if the stick was mitigated by the occasional carrot?'

'Wasn't it?'

She didn't see it this time, only sensed the bleakness tingeing the air.

'He reserved his affections for others. One person in particular. A person who didn't particularly welcome it.'

Having been a subject of blatant favouritism, Lauren could hazard a guess. 'Your brother?'

'No.' The terse response came without further clarification.

'Who, then?'

A firmer flattening of his lips, then, 'My mother,' he rasped.

She frowned, recalling that while he'd spoken of his brother and father, he'd rarely mentioned his mother. In fact, was it only yesterday he'd spoken of her? She felt as if she'd lived a year since they'd met in his office.

'Does she live with you at the palace?'

'No.'

The finality of the answer made her wonder if she'd drawn a bad memory. 'I'm sorry, she's not... is she still...?'

'Alive? Yes, very much so. She moved to Paris after my father died. We meet once or twice a year for the customary stilted lunch or dinner when she stages a maternal performance neither of us believe in.'

Lauren winced at the acerbity in his tone. 'Why staged?'

His nostrils gave the briefest flare, then he was back in supreme control. 'Because my mother exists solely to bargain her way into more of whatever she desires.' He caught her puzzled frown and elaborated. 'She isn't the kind of mother who gives anything for free, be it her duties as Queen Mother or her affection for her children.'

'You mean she had to be *paid* to love you?' she asked, disbelief bleeding through her voice.

Another stark look flashed across his face. 'Is it love if she had to be paid to bear me or my brother?'

'How do you know? Did she…did she tell you?' The thought of that was abhorrent, even worse in her opinion than being abandoned at birth by a mother who wanted nothing to do with you. At least in her case, she'd been given up to the authorities in the hope that she might be given a better life.

'There was documentation to that effect. She received a sum for delivering her firstborn and another for her second. From then on, each achievement, great or small, was transactional. I learned that to get her attention, I needed to give her something in return.'

'Something like what?'

'As a child it was mostly a sacrificial transaction. One appearance at a school recital meant she was free to skip the next two or three. As an adult, it was more…materialistic. Attending a handful of important state functions usually cost me a villa in Spain or an upgrade on her private jet.'

She sucked in a stunned breath. 'That's…deplorable.'

'Is it?' he parried with a curiously flat tone. 'Or was it a valuable early lesson that everything comes at a price?'

'Surely you don't believe that?'

Leonine eyes cut to her, their depths holding no give. 'Isn't that why you're here? You may delude yourself that it is out of duty for your brother, but haven't others bargained with that duty to drive you to me when it was perhaps not your own choice?'

His intuitiveness floored her, as did the cutting comparison to his mother. But in truth, she could deny neither.

She was still floundering when he clicked his tongue and muttered to his mount. The camel kicked into a light trot, signalling their conversation was over. Hers followed, uneasy silence descending as they headed north.

Just as she feared her nerves would snap at the tension between them, a stunning, immense riad-style villa came into view. With soaring gold sun-shaped domes and ochre exterior walls, it blended seamlessly into the desert.

As they drew closer, she saw further graceful arches and wide terraces, the breathtaking Moorish villa a feast for the senses. Guards were posted at the entrance and at various discreet points along the storeyed terraces, but it didn't take away from the beauty of Tahir's desert residence.

It was only as Lauren's gaze shifted back to Tahir's broad shoulders that she realised they were bypassing the entrance and skirting the villa altogether.

Another handful of minutes later, they approached a wide cluster of palm trees and what looked astonishingly like…a large, sparkling body of water.

She reached him just as his camel was settling itself on the ground and Tahir was sliding out of his saddle.

'Where are we?'

'My private oasis. We'll go inside once we're done here.'

He murmured to her mount and the creature lowered itself. Her breath locked in her throat when he reached for her. As before, he wrapped his hands around her waist and lifted her off the beast, but this time they faced one another, and the strong compulsion that seemed to have become part of her commanded her gaze upward to clash with his.

For breathless moments, they simply stared at one another, his hands holding her captive while her heart banged hard against her ribs. Perhaps it was a trick of the light, but everything inside her froze in anticipation as his head descended a fraction, those far too sensual lips drawing tantalisingly closer.

But in the next instant he was setting her free, jerking away from her before striding towards his guards. One of them approached with a large basket and set it down on a flat rock a few feet from the edge of the water as she took a better look at her surroundings.

Several tall boulders formed a natural barrier against the elements on one side, while palm trees framed the remaining area, creating a circle of rock and trees with the sparkling spring a welcoming respite stop.

The spring itself was about the size of two Olympic-sized swimming pools and as she approached it she could see clear to the bottom of the turquoise-coloured water.

'I usually come to cool off here to complete my journey,' Tahir murmured from behind her.

She startled a little, unaware he'd approached while she'd been lost in the wonder of the little oasis. Then all she could think of was him, his proximity wreaking havoc on her senses.

'It's beautiful. It feels like a special place.' A place for lovers. For a sheikh to relax with his sheikha. To forget about duty and obligations and destiny and simply…be.

And because she knew such a place would never be for her with a man like Tahir, she cast around for a way, *any* way to distract herself from the acutely depressing thought.

But then he stepped away, and she saw that they were alone. The bodyguards had left. It was most likely because there was only one entrance to this magical place, and they were confident their sire wouldn't be in any danger.

'This is the only place I'm truly alone.'

'Do you want me here?' Her gaze went to where the contents of the basket had been spread out on a large picnic blanket. Somehow, the hourglass was still upright, the passage of time relentless. Peering closer, she saw that there was about a quarter of the portion remaining. 'You can have the rest of the time on your own.'

'I said twenty-four hours together. Nothing has changed.'

She swallowed her disquiet. 'What would you do if you were here on your own?'

A glimmer started in his eyes, and she watched, breath held tight in her chest, as it grew to a spark, then a flame. She was half relieved, half disappointed when his lashes dropped but it was only so he could conduct a searing scrutiny of her body, in a way that left little doubt as to the direction of his thoughts. The sensations roiling through her gave way to hot, scalding jealousy. Was he thinking about the last time he'd been here and, specifically, who he'd been with?

'Never mind. I don't think I want to know.'

Both eyebrows slowly rose. 'Oh, but I think you do,' he drawled.

'What you do and who you do it with is none of my business.'

'Then why ask?'

She floundered, then threw in a shrug. 'I was just making conversation.'

'You've come this far. Don't be a coward now, *habibti*.'

Habibti. She knew that word. It was an endearment she hadn't heard in a dozen years. Last whispered hotly in her ear, right before a hoarse roar signalled his climax swiftly on the heels of hers.

Darling. Sweetheart. Treasured one.

The spark of heat in her blood became a blaze, charged by the memory and his deliberate taunt. Calling her a coward was meant to rile her. She knew that. She shouldn't have fallen for it.

And yet she let him stoke the fire. Let her nostrils flare in a fruitless exhale of her irritation. 'Call me a coward again. I dare you. *Your Majesty.*' She let her own taunt linger in his title, felt a bolt of satisfaction when his eyes narrowed.

'Here in this place, I'm Tahir to you. And *you* can be your true self. No inhibitions.'

Those last two words turned that blaze into an inferno. Something dangerously sultry and seductive that magnified the thumping of her heart; intensified the sweet, heavy scents weaving through the air. The very tangible thrum of lust winding around them.

Without waiting for a response—or because he wasn't about to be affected one way or the other by whatever she did next—he strolled with sure, lithe strides towards the waterfall.

'You asked what I normally do here when I'm alone. I would normally swim naked. But so as not to excite your very English sensibilities…' He deliberately trailed off, absorbing every ounce of his attention as he pulled the strings of his trousers and the linen material dropped to pool at his feet.

Lauren was half ashamed of the dart of disappointment when she saw the boxer shorts he wore beneath. The other half of her was desperately pleading with herself to stop her blatant ogling of his magnificent body.

As was evident from watching him this last half-day, the years had only built on the already perfect specimen that was Tahir Al-Jukrat.

There was no spare flesh on his body, just a physique honed by genes and discipline and a masculinity gifted by an impeccable lineage.

The blazing sun threw every bare inch of him into perfect, bronzed relief and a full-bodied shiver tingled through her, a deep craving to touch seizing her with such power that she needed to yank her gaze away to stop herself from doing the unthinkable. From surging up and closing the distance between them, letting her fingers explore the chiselled planes and muscled valleys. From scenting and tasting and feasting as she never had before.

A loud splash jerked her free of her desperate craving to find Tahir submerged in the crystal-clear water. He dived beneath the surface, causing barely a ripple. She held her breath, watching with rapt attention as half a minute passed before he broke the surface at the far end.

'Are you just going to sit there?'

His deep, sexy voice carried across the water, made all the more electrifying by the look he cast her.

Lauren chewed on her lip.

A swim with the sovereign ruler of Jukrat. Something to tell her grandchildren decades from now when she reprised the twenty-four-hour game she'd engaged in with Tahir.

For the sake of her brother.

Guilt rippled through her chest. She hadn't given Matt a thought in the last hour. Watching Tahir's lazy, powerful strokes as he swam back to her, she knew she wouldn't be thinking about her brother for the duration of the time in the hourglass.

'I don't have a swimsuit,' she said, clinging to the feeble excuse.

He resurfaced a few feet from her, throwing his head back to dislodge the wet strands from his eyes. The move threw his face and throat into sun-worshipping relief, and it was so sexy, Lauren couldn't help but stare in awe. Even when his gaze settled on her, when he drifted closer, his eyes darkening with the desire he seemed to be giving free rein to, she couldn't avert her gaze.

'Are you going to let that stop you?'

She grimaced at the thought of swimming in her underwear. But the superseding thought was that she would be minus the cover of her clothes, in the presence of the most dynamic, physically arresting man she'd ever encountered.

And why that only sent spirals of fevered anticipation through her veins.

She'd covered her head and shoulders with the wrap before they'd left the camp and now the sun had risen higher, it was a relief to discard it. Especially when Tahir's gaze heated up as it raked the skin she bared.

Breath hitching, she dropped her gaze from his, striving not to be overwhelmed as she eased down the zip beneath one arm and drew the top over her head. Rising to her feet, she pulled off the skirt and tossed it away.

Tahir's gaze was still locked on her when she sent a furtive glance his way, and she couldn't stop the flow of heat to her face at the stamp of arousal etched into his.

With a smooth dive, she plunged into the water, with hope she suspected was futile that it would dissipate the reciprocal sensations moving through her.

For a few moments, she was overcome with a different sensation.

Her bath last night had been heavenly, but this was pure bliss. Copying Tahir, she swam underwater until her lungs demanded oxygen.

When she surfaced, he was resting against the rock she'd just dived off, his elbows propped behind him as he watched her.

She told herself the distance was wise. And yet, a few minutes later, she found herself drifting towards him, her gaze locked on him.

'Enjoying yourself?' he drawled, a glint in his eyes.

She was, and again that dart of guilt assailed her. The glint disappeared, his eyes turning brooding again. 'This is my time, and I will not permit self-flagellation. Especially when the cause is your brother,' he growled.

'You mean to command my emotions now?' It slipped out before she could stop herself, that thrilling urge to challenge him a lure she couldn't resist.

'You think I cannot?' he returned. Before she could respond, 'Come here, Lauren,' he growled, eyes fixed on her with rabid intensity.

She shook her head but even that action was too feeble for her liking.

He didn't address her refusal, merely continued to stare at her with heavy, imperious expectation.

Wondrously compelled, she complied, her actions almost independent of her stunned thoughts. She reached him, and witnessed the infuriating satisfaction etched in his face.

Spinning her around with speed that snatched her breath away, he lifted her from the water, settled her on the flat rock and dropped his forearms on both sides of her hips.

Lauren fought the urge to fidget, fought the urge to demand he put those hands on her. Because in that moment, nothing else mattered but satisfying the clarion call of her body, the demand to lick off those droplets of water saucily clinging to his lips.

She must have made a sound or licked her own lips; Lauren couldn't summon the cognition to verify. His eyes dropped to her mouth, his jaw clenching tight as he exhaled harshly.

Gripping the backs of her thighs, he parted her legs and situated himself between them. The hard, packed torso brushed her inner thighs as he moved closer. Heated eyes scoured her body once. Twice. Then a low growl rumbled from him. 'I have to taste you again.'

Anticipation shivered through her as she too exhaled. 'Please,' she whispered, too far gone to contemplate the consequences of that one, betraying word.

Flames burst to life in his eyes, sending out a loud warning that she might not be the same once he was done accepting the invitation she'd issued.

'Be sure, Lauren,' he added, as if he'd divined the inner caution.

In answer, and because her roiling senses had deprived her of speech, she draped her arms around his neck, then lowered her head until their lips were less than an inch apart.

The invitation was clear. Unequivocal.

He seized it.

The hands she'd craved clutched at her hips, digging in and branding her and holding her in place. At the same time, he surged up and captured her mouth with his in a deep ravishing that had her moaning with pleasure.

His tongue swept into her mouth, tangling briefly with hers before he nipped at her bottom lip. Her tiny cry drew an animalistic groan from his throat. Then he was swirling his tongue over the delicious hurt, creating whirlpools of desire that swiftly turned into ravenous cyclones. Her fingers tunnelled into his wet hair, gripping tight as she strained closer.

Her breasts pressed into his chest, the diamond-hard tips causing decadent friction that intensified the flames leaping through her blood. Between her legs, damp heat mounted, her clitoris plumping in needy longing.

Again and again, he nipped and licked and devoured.

Again and again, she shuddered in delight, her senses soaring. She'd lost sense of time when he raised his head, pulling back a fraction.

A whimper escaped her. 'More,' she pleaded. Drunk on desire. Drunk on him.

For an eternity, his gaze drilled into hers, seeking something she couldn't quite name. After another eternity, he dragged her arms from his neck and planted them on the rock.

'Don't move,' he commanded.

She was about to protest the distance between them, her breath strangled when he surged forward, his mouth locating the pulse throbbing at her throat. Another helpless cry fell from her lips, echoing over the water before surging back into her. Her vision grew hazy, delight dancing through her.

Languidly, he explored her pulse, basking in the furious desire he'd created in her.

His fingers moved to her bra strap. Still trailing his lips over her skin, he lowered one, then the other. Firm lips brushed her collarbone and a deep sigh escaped her.

She'd missed this.

Missed *him*.

This mindless pleasure only he had been able to invoke in her. It dawned on her then that the reason she hadn't been able to commit to the few relationships she'd tried out was because they'd never come close to what she'd experienced with Tahir. Neither time nor experience had brought the sort of exhilarating combustion just being in Tahir's presence had provoked. And so, she'd given up even before it'd started…

For one heart-thumping moment the power of that realisation threatened to wrench her from the euphoria engulfing her. But then his masterful lips trailed lower, over the crest of her breast, and she was lost. In sensation. In stomach-clenching anticipation as he dropped kisses over her flesh, everywhere but where she needed him most. The hard peak furled tighter as she clenched her fingers in his hair, urging him to her nipple.

It was only because her rapt gaze was fixed on him that she caught his fleeting, wicked smile. But his face grew serious again, the hard edge of arousal making him even more breathtaking. Making her insides melt with disgraceful ease.

She was watching him when those lips closed over one rosy peak. He boldly suckled her, swirled his tongue in decadent flickers that arrowed sensation straight between her legs.

Lauren gave herself up to the pleasure, panting when, after mindless minutes, he firmly urged her backwards to lie flat on the stone.

Brooding eyes skimmed greedily over her, setting off further fireworks wherever it touched.

'You look like the most decadent sacrifice, *habibti*.'

She wanted to ask if such a sacrifice was worthy to erase the turbulent episode of their past.

But desire and emotion she wasn't willing to name clogged her throat. Perhaps that was a good thing because she didn't want to ruin this moment. Didn't want to halt this incredible experience that might very well be her last.

Right now, Lauren was fully intent on being selfish. On not allowing thoughts of Matt or her parents to impinge on this moment.

She took it without shame or rancour. Because it was possible this might be what she needed to move on. To form better relationships in the future.

Her actions had prevented them from reaching the natural conclusion of their last affair. Perhaps this was the closure she needed.

Or maybe you're deluding yourself.

She shied away from the taunting voice, happily gave up thinking as Tahir spoke again.

'A sacrifice I won't deny myself,' he concluded

thickly, his hands tightening on her inner thighs. Right before he parted her to his searing gaze.

For another interminable age, he simply stared down at her, his tongue moving languidly over his bottom lip in shameless, ravenous anticipation.

'Tahir.' His name was a croak of helpless need that had his nostrils flaring in satisfaction and triumph. That had his broad shoulders squaring as if accepting his regal due.

'Yes, *habibti*. You will say my name like that, scream it when I bring you pleasure.'

Another imperious command she had no trouble obeying.

And when he lowered his head and boldly tasted her, she cried out, her head rolling back as desire rippled in relentless waves through her.

He teased and tormented, savoured and pleasured her until his name was an anthem, her hands blindly seeking his broad shoulders as he pushed her to the brink.

The sweet torment intensified as he kept her there, repeatedly denying her release until she was a mindless mess.

Only then did he grant her the climax that had her screaming his name, her nails digging into his flesh as bliss washed over her.

Eyes squeezed shut, her breathing rapid enough to cause alarm, she felt him climb onto the rock beside her, gather her close.

Still drunk on her release, she burrowed into

him, the warmth and scent of his skin filling her with further delight.

But soon the silence encroached, the fractious past and unstable present splintering the air in the aftermath.

She wanted to raise her head, look into his face and decipher what he was thinking but, again, she feared what he would read in hers.

So when, without speaking, he slipped off the rock and lowered them both into the water, she told herself it was for the best. When he swam to the other side, heaved himself out of the water and began to dress, she convinced herself there was no reason to be upset.

And yet, upset she was as she too dressed, and they picnicked in silence. As she let him lift her back onto the camel to complete their journey.

He shouldn't have done that.

The grim conclusion settled deeper into Tahir as they dressed. For starters, he'd created a memory he'd now always associate with Lauren at a place special to him.

He'd given in to temptation.

He exhaled in self-loathing and self-recrimination.

Mere hours after he'd proclaimed such a thing would never happen, he'd jumped into the fire of desire that now threatened to consume him. He grimaced and adjusted the painful throbbing of his arousal. To compound his sins, he couldn't stop glancing her way. Couldn't stop his eyes lingering on lips reddened from his kisses. From examining the faint marks he'd left on her neck with his heavy caresses as she half-heartedly nibbled fruit from their picnic spread.

Steering his gaze away for the umpteenth time, he willed calm into his body, dredged up all the reasons why tangling with her was a bad idea.

But those reasons felt hollow when all he could concentrate on were her moans, her eager responses and those greedy hands on his body.

Tahir was relieved when he finally guided her to his riad.

Home.

Yet another place he was bringing Lauren to that held the potential to etch memories he didn't want added to the fabric of his life.

The solution is easy. End this now. Send her away.

His unfettered growl made the camel corralled nearby grunt uneasily.

Reaching out, he smoothed his hand down the camel's side. 'Easy, *habibti*,' he murmured, then grimaced. Another endearment he couldn't utter without thinking about her and what had just occurred.

Her uninhibited responses. That tinge of wonder that made him speculate what sort of relation-

ships she'd been in that could've left such traces of
innocence.

He growled again as another sensation stirred
within him.

Jealousy.

Ridiculous, he told himself. He was a sheikh, the
supreme ruler of a prosperous kingdom.

True. But he'd been drawn to this one right from
the start.

Yes. And she betrayed you. Remember that.

Curiously though, the insistence was less powerful, the hint of a question at the end of that warning disturbing enough for him to quicken his steps,
hoping it would dispel the thoughts pursuing him.

Yes, Lauren might have betrayed him. They
would never be friends but how many of his past
lovers had he been friends with?

His jaw clenched as he summed up the number
on one hand. As his mother had taught him, he'd
ensured his liaisons were transactional. Guaran-
teed pleasure on both sides, followed by a tasteful
gift and assurance that the involvement would remain discreet.

*And that was a thing to be proud of? Like bar-
ing the details of his relationship with his parents,
something he'd never discussed with anyone but
his younger brother?*

He swallowed as his discomfort intensified, as
the true depths of his revelations settled on him.
Lauren was the only woman he'd acted out of char-

acter with. Should she choose to make public the intimate details he'd shared with her as she had twelve years ago, he would deal with it.

With compulsion he was starting to resent, his gaze swung back to her.

What was it about this woman that made him act out of character? It couldn't simply be her ravishing body. Her brilliant mind had also been a thing of awe.

But he'd met equally brilliant people in his time as Prince and many more since he took the throne. None of them had impacted him so deeply.

So what was it…?

He gladly gave up pursuing his chaotic thoughts as he walked through the gates of the sprawling riad.

This time when he helped Lauren off her camel, he ensured there was minimal contact, striding off the moment her feet touched the ground. He curled the hands that itched to touch her, relive those moments at the springs, and took a step back.

'You'll be shown to your rooms to refresh, but the game isn't done. See you in ten minutes.'

CHAPTER SEVEN

LAUREN WATCHED HIM walk away, her thoughts churning faster with each step he took away from her. As at the camp, beautifully dressed female attendants surrounded her, the matron introducing herself as Nesa.

Unlike the desert, however, these women were less smiley, the contemplative curiosity in their eyes more solemn than their nomadic counterparts. They also moved with purposeful briskness, ushering her away with quick, firm strides.

Lauren felt like a goldfish in a bowl as she trotted after them, her eyes goggling at her stunning surroundings.

Several arched mosaic-tiled hallways bordered large courtyards overflowing with potted palms, cacti and colourful groupings of seats.

After the sixth such courtyard, she knew she'd need a map to navigate her way around the villa.

They finally stopped before a set of soaring double doors made entirely of what looked like carved petrified wood. Had she been alone, Lauren was sure she'd have run her fingers over it, explored the gentle bumps and dips carved by time and the deep gold handles in wonder.

But then she was being ushered into a breathtakingly beautiful private living room. On the floors, large, exquisite Persian and Berber rugs muffled the sound of their footsteps. The ocean-blue colour scheme was repeated in the velvet sofa, the multitude of cushions and benches stationed around the room and the mosaic patterns etched into the walls and ceilings.

A queen-sized bed was equally exquisite, with posts and white muslin curtains currently drawn back and held by silk woven rope. On the opposite side of the dressing room, she was beckoned by another colourful room.

The walls of the bathroom were painted a jewelled peacock green with gold and copper accents including a large tub that made her yearn for a dip. Dragging her gaze from the inviting sight, she followed through into a dressing room, slowing to stop at the sight that greeted her.

No.

Tahir wouldn't be so crass as to direct his staff to show her into a room that belonged to a lover or concubine.

Nevertheless, she needed to be sure. The mixture of dread and jealousy stirring in her stomach would only grow if she remained silent.

'I think there's been a mistake. These clothes...' She paused, wondering how to couch her words without causing offence. 'They're not mine.'

'His Majesty's residences maintain a certain

standard,' Nesa replied. 'I'm sure he wouldn't like for any guest to feel...inconvenienced.'

Lauren sensed criticism within the words but strove to rise above it.

Delivering a saccharine smile of her own—a talent she'd honed from years of dealing with sketchy politicians with hidden agendas—she nodded. 'Thank you for the consideration.'

Nesa inclined her head, and just like that the matter was settled. They showed her the balcony with the trellised pergola that boasted even more areas for relaxation and after another stolen minute admiring the jaw-dropping views of mountains and sand dunes, she returned to the bedroom, freezing when she saw the phone on the bedside table.

'Do you have mobile service here?'

Her heart fell as Nesa shook her head. 'No, but the landline works.'

She barely heard Nesa say she would fetch her in five minutes. The moment Lauren was alone, she hurried to the phone. Heart in her mouth, she lifted the receiver and dialled the familiar number.

'Hello?'

'Lauren?' Her mother's cultured tones held underlying censure and disapproval. 'Where have you been? The staff have been trying to reach you at your hotel since yesterday.'

The staff.

Not her. Not her father. No enquiries as to whether she was okay.

Despite three decades of the tangible distance she'd always felt from her parents, her stupid, vulnerable craving for acceptance made it hurt that neither of them had bothered to pick up the phone themselves.

She gripped the handset tighter and buried the hurt, as she was used to doing. 'There was no time to let you know where I was going.'

'And where did you go?' Alice Winchester enquired. 'Did you manage to make progress with Matt's case?'

'Not yet.'

'Not yet,' her mother echoed, a distinct chill in her voice. 'You've been there four days.'

I'm not a miracle worker, she wanted to snap. She bit her tongue just in time to hear her mother sniff.

'Poor Matt must be beside himself.'

'Have you spoken to him?'

A throb of silence passed before her mother answered, 'I've been told he's not allowed phone calls.'

It wasn't true. Her mother simply hadn't been able to fit in a call to her jailed son around her schedule. Or more likely, her father had forbidden her from contacting Matt in case word got out.

'We'll have ample time to speak when he gets home. You are making sure that happens, aren't you?' The question was pointed, the ever-present implication that Lauren wasn't allowed to fail heavily underscored.

Her gaze went to the empty doorway, for some absurd reason picturing Tahir standing there with another brooding look levelled her way. Heat snaked through her, her mind delving back to what had happened at the springs, how much she'd given up to him, consequences be damned—

'Lauren? Are you there?'

She started guiltily, controlling her erratic breathing as she answered, 'I'm here, Mum. And...yes, I'm working on it.'

'Good. Your father will be glad to hear that. We really need to put this unpleasant business behind us as soon as possible. Let us know when you're both on your way home.' The final words held a throb of hope laced with guilt, and she wondered whether her mother felt more than she was projecting.

Before Lauren could be certain, the line went dead. She replaced the receiver as Tahir's words from last night echoed in her mind.

'...why you're sacrificing yourself for the sake of your ungrateful family.'

The question prodded harder as she stared at herself in the bathroom mirror.

Her braid had come loose during her swim. Locating a brush, she dragged it through the tresses until they flowed over her shoulders. Aware that the minutes were fast ticking down, she hurried to the dressing room and plucked out the first outfit she saw.

The cobalt-blue skirt was the same layered Jukrati design she'd worn last night, but with a wide-sleeved matching top. The material was a soft, light and airy linen, the exaggerated boat-shaped design of the top allowing for her healing shoulder burns not to be aggravated.

Sliding on slippers in the same hue, she dug out her lip gloss from her handbag and applied a light sheen before leaving her bed suite.

Nesa was waiting on a delicate-looking scroll bench outside her rooms, her arms folded neatly in her lap. When she saw Lauren, she rose and politely gestured towards another arched hallway.

They passed Doric columns and walls decorated with Arabian lanterns that threw artful shapes onto the walls, making the whole space a feast for the eyes and the senses.

Another myriad hallways, tiny alcoves and courtyards later, they arrived in the largest space she'd seen yet.

It was a garden courtyard, the largest one she'd seen so far and it was stunning, the peacock-green walls and trees decorated with miniature Turkish lamps that would be spectacular in the evening. In true Jukrati style, low divans and long benches festooned with bright-coloured cushions were positioned in careful arrangements. In one corner, a small fountain tinkled pleasantly, adding a relaxing ambience to the space.

Seeing Tahir seated at one of the tables didn't

exactly aid that relaxation though. Hysterical butterflies took wing in her belly, their agitation in-
tensifying the closer she got to him.

He'd changed attire too, and if his all-black gar-
ments from last night had given him a larger-than-
life presence, his all-white tunic and trousers now
lent him a towering aura that was far too breathtaking.

He watched her for a beat before he spoke. 'You
spoke to your parents.'

It wasn't a question. Anger and hurt—most likely
a residue from her phone call with her mother—
lashed within her. 'You're monitoring my calls?'

'Do I need to remind you again of my security
protocols?' Before she could answer, he continued
coolly, 'A call was logged to England. The content
of your call wasn't monitored. I drew the natural
conclusion.'

As quickly as it rose, her temper dissipated.
'Okay. Yes, I spoke with my mother.'

One eyebrow slowly rose. 'By your tone, the conversation didn't go the way you imagined it would?'

She wanted to snap at him not to make her relive
it. But that was as good as admitting things were
bad. That she was burying her head in the sand.
And…she was tired of doing that. Tired of fighting on endless fronts.

'No, it didn't.'

He stared at her for an age, then, without breaking eye contact, he raised his hand. Seeming to

materialise out of thin air, a smiling young man stepped forward with a tray of refreshments. 'Lunch will be served in two hours. In the meantime, have something. You barely ate the picnic food.'

The reminder of their torrid episode at the springs drew heat into her face. She remained silent as a bountiful spread was laid out on the table.

Then the now familiar hourglass tray was delivered on a hand-painted pedestal and placed next to her chair.

'Shall we resume?'

He was sticking to the letter of their game, but she had a strong feeling he would be counting the minutes until he took full control again.

When she lifted the silk cloth, a mere fifteen minutes stood between her and his wish. Resolutely, she flipped the hourglass. And took a different tack.

'Are you going to tell me what the problem is in Riyaal?'

For the longest time, his lips firmed. Just when she thought he'd refuse to answer, he did. 'My cousin is being obstinate about our trade talks. Apparently, he's decided the terms aren't quite to his liking even though we agreed on them months ago.'

'And you can't hold him to them?'

Tahir exhaled in frustration. 'I've just learned he's made bad deals with a few other states, made promises he couldn't keep and now it's beginning to impact his deal with me.'

'How?' she asked, a little too eagerly.

'His levies are crushing him, and he's making threats about passing them on to me.' He paused, his eyes narrowing on her. 'How would you deal with this?'

Her eyebrows shot up while eddies of warmth sprang up inside her. 'You want my input?'

He shrugged. 'I find that not every answer can be arrived at with linear thinking. The obvious answer is to refuse and let him stick to our original agreement, of course. But perhaps you have another solution?'

'You automatically assume my reasoning is going to be radical?'

A twitch that wasn't quite a smile flashed at one corner of his lip. 'I recall a few instances when you've adopted such a stance successfully.'

Tahir watched her contemplate his response.

Did she realise she was drawing closer? That the spark she'd claimed she'd wilfully abandoned was right there in her eyes? That she'd adopted that challenging posture that made his blood rush a little too fast through his veins because he knew he was in for a heated debate with a woman who thrived on such verbal skirmishes?

This was the woman he remembered. And for good or ill, the impulse to reawaken her was why he'd summoned her parents to Jukrat. For his own peace of mind, this matter would be settled once and for all with the woman who wasn't a shadow of herself.

Is that the true reason?

Tahir held himself still and reassured himself that it was.

But it was a lie that shook through him with far more fervour than he welcomed. 'Let's hear it, then,' he said briskly, hoping his stern tone would shake off the other disconcerting emotions weaving through him.

Lauren berated herself for her foolish heart skipping several beats. Tahir was merely seeking an opinion—probably one of many—not planning to base his entire life model on it. Nonetheless, she couldn't quite halt the thrill snaking through her.

'Has he done something like this to you before?'

'In varying degrees but nothing this drastic before now.' Tahir's lips twisted. 'Unfortunately, more often than not, asking Adnan to keep a promise is like placing a sweet in a toddler's hand and asking them not to eat it.'

'What are you going to do?'

A chilling smile curved his lips, triggering the reminder the blood of marauders ran through his veins. 'I've tried the velvet gloves, perhaps it's time for the steel hammer.'

She pursed her lips. His eyes narrowed on her. 'You disapprove,' he surmised. Then before she could respond, he pushed. 'You have an alternative?'

'Maybe.'

'I'm listening.'

Why did that please her enough to make her heart leap? 'Put him in a position where he has no option but to do the right thing.'

He grimaced. 'How? He's as intransigent as they come. He digs his heels in even when it's not necessary just to be bloody-minded.'

'People like that often do it for the attention. He probably craves yours.'

'I can't pander to him just to make him behave himself,' he grunted.

'But dragging things out indefinitely will not just hurt him, it'll hurt you too in the long run. Make him an offer he can't refuse.'

A frown creased his forehead for a full minute. 'He's found himself in this position because he's brash and impetuous. His policies often fail because they're rarely thought through efficiently.'

'So he could benefit from some guidance? From someone like your brother? In a different advisory role, perhaps?' His lips flattened and Lauren knew he didn't like the idea. 'You won't have to lose your brother's diplomatic services. But having a man like Javid in his corner might be just what brings him around?'

Slowly his scowl cleared. 'I may not have had much time for him when we were younger, but he got on well enough with Javid. And there's no reason why Javid can't continue his duties alongside.

Perhaps that might even curb some of his less sa-
lubrious activities,' he mused with a throb of satisfaction in his voice.

'There you go, then. Problem solved.' Lauren
wasn't aware she was smiling until his eyes scoured
her face and dropped to linger on her mouth.

'Indeed. How alive you come when you're in
your element.'

Something passed between them…a potent connection that stole her breath for several seconds
before delivering a heart pounding she knew she
should ignore.

But on the tail of it, that disquieting sensation
lingered until she knew she had to air it. 'Tahir…
this latest thing with Adnan isn't happening because
of…my presence, is it?' His nostrils flared, and she
wanted to kick herself for ruining the atmosphere.
'I'm sorry, but I have to know—'

'Whether he's caught wind of my ex-lover's arrival and believes I'm distracted?' His lips firmed.
'Probably. Spies don't just exist in movies and nov-
els.'

'But you don't know for sure?'

'Leave me to handle my cousin. But be assured
that neither he nor your brother will interrupt the
remainder of our twenty-four hours,' he clipped out.

Frantically, she tore her gaze from him, feigning
interest in the beauty and magic of the place so he
wouldn't see how affected she was by the reminder
of their limited time.

But then she forced herself to be realistic. It would take more than half a day to erase what had happened twelve years ago, especially when she hadn't come fully clean.

Biting her lip, she concentrated more on her surroundings, letting them wash over her. 'It's beautiful and peaceful here,' she murmured, tactfully changing the subject.

A throb of silence passed, during which his gaze remained fixed on her, before he replied. 'It wasn't always.'

Her heart thudded heavily in her chest. 'Because of your banishment?'

'Yes.'

Lauren decided to forge ahead to the subject that weighed heavier on her mind and heart with each passing minute. 'I hate that I contributed to turning something you loved into an unpleasant memory for you.'

He looked around him for several seconds before he answered. 'It was a good lesson in not taking things for granted or at face value.'

That stung far more than the pragmatism in his response should've elicited. 'Maybe. But did you really need another reminder? And did that reminder have to be this one?'

'We can't change the past, Lauren,' he said with a finality that shook her to her very bones.

'No, but you can consider forgiving it,' she murmured.

His nostrils pinched but he continued to regard her like a specimen under a microscope. 'Convince me that there's more than one reason for you being here. Do that, and I'll consider it,' he countered smoothly, one contemplative finger trailing the lip of his coffee cup. But underneath it, there was fierce tension that jangled her nerves.

What he was asking of her…

She'd bared so much of herself and been hurt in the process by the family that should've loved her.

But wasn't she tired? Wasn't enough quite enough?

Lauren dragged her gaze from the sensual motion of his finger and sucked in a breath. This time, she wasn't frantic at the relentless passage of time. Because while her first reaction was to say *no* to this question, deep inside, another response burned within her.

Of course, he gleaned that with his next words. 'You won't be betraying him by admitting Matt is long overdue a few life lessons. And you're equally overdue a little reconditioning of your own.'

She played it cool, arching a lazy eyebrow. 'Such as?'

'You throttle your ambition and desires for a family that doesn't appreciate you. At the risk of repeating myself, you're wasted on them. Your talent, your passion.' His burnished gaze raked her face, lingering on her mouth. 'Your beauty.' The thick, peculiar note in his voice burrowed deep inside her, warmed her where she'd grown used to being so cold it'd become a part of her.

But the thawing was painful, the admission that change was needed lodging a huge lump in her throat. 'You can't change your family. You know that as well as I do. What would you have me do?' she tossed back, not quite ready to confront the solution that shrieked in her head.

He regarded her steadily with far too much circumspection in his gaze. 'You know, Lauren,' he delivered without pomp or gloating. 'You've always known. You were abandoned by your mother so you're afraid you'll be abandoned again.'

She gasped. 'You know I was adopted?'

Tawny eyes met hers and she saw neither judgement nor rejection. 'Yes. Matt told me years ago,' he replied, then, before she could absorb that news, he was moving on. As if it was no big deal. 'You're strong. Don't subdue your own strength just to make them feel stronger. Step out from the shadows. Remind yourself how it feels to bask in the light. How it feels to let go and just…feel.'

It spoke volumes of her need that she was immediately thrown back to their time at his oasis when she'd vowed she wasn't going to think about the pleasure he'd given her at the springs. Not just physical pleasure but a connection she hadn't felt in years.

Dear God, she wanted a repeat performance.

Wanted reprieve—and not just a temporary one, her heart insisted—from those shadows he spoke of.

She pushed away the lingering guilt over Matt.

She would never be in this place again, would probably never share space with Tahir, so why not let the time unfold without the angst and tension? Why not come clean with everything and let the chips fall where they might? Drawing a deep breath, she looked him in the eyes. 'Those shadows you talked about…some of them were because of you.'

He stiffened. 'What?'

'I…you probably don't remember but there were texts…besides the photos?'

His eyes darkened to burnished gold. 'I remember.'

She gasped softly. 'You do?'

'Yes. What about them, Lauren?' he pressed, a sharp edge in his voice.

'My phone went missing…after the pictures were leaked. I never found it. But…' She paused, unable to put her suspicions into words. To do so would be to damn her family definitively.

'But you think you know who has it? Let me guess, one of your family?'

Anguish mounting, she nodded.

He exhaled slowly, his expression growing livid. 'Let me get this straight. You thought they may have got their hands on something that would cause a nuisance and you let them hold it over your head?'

Her hand tightened around her cup. 'It was more than a nuisance. You were already caught in one scandal and—'

'And the far worse damage was already done, Lauren.'

'No, it wasn't. I couldn't risk it.'

He shook his head. 'Pictures of a prince doctored to suggest he was involved with a sex and drugs party are a world away from a few racy texts exchanged with his lover, don't you agree?'

'Then why do you look so angry?'

He muttered an Arabic imprecation under his breath. Then he was cupping her nape, drawing her close. Hot, demanding lips sealed hers, his tongue breaching her lips to dance sinfully with hers in a kiss that left them both breathless when he pulled away several minutes later.

Senses spinning, every cell in her body hungering for more, she pressed her fingers against his throbbing lips before demanding, 'What was that for?'

'It was a choice between that and putting you over my knee and spanking the hell out of you for diminishing yourself in a misguided notion that you were saving me. This king is perfectly able to handle nuisances like that.'

Her mouth gaped, and she wasn't sure whether his words scandalised her or turned her on. 'I… you're unbelievable.'

An enigmatic expression flitted through his eyes.

'And you're forgiven,' he clipped out. Before her heart could leap with joy, he added, 'For that at least.'

The bubble of hope dying inside, she veiled her gaze.

Until he grasped her chin, nudged her to meet his eyes. 'Back to our previous discussion. Are you ready to shed those shadows?' he demanded thickly.

She wasn't but the temptation to *just feel* as he'd urged was irresistible. 'Does that mean we dispense with the hourglasses?' she asked eventually.

He shook his head, and she watched the sunlight dance over the gloss of his jet-black hair, watched it create intriguing shadows over his face. 'Oh, no. Those stay. Far be it from you to level an accusation of inequality on me come morning. Besides, I suspect you're quite enjoying our little game?'

Heaven help her but she was. With vibrant new clothes, her surroundings and the breathtakingly powerful, charismatic King for company, it was as close to the fairy tales she'd devoured as a child as she imagined she would get.

She didn't want to think about her present or her life back in London. She wanted to remain locked in this moment with Tahir, when the only thing she needed to concentrate on was when those elegant hands would pluck the next silk covering off the hourglass, and what that might hold in store for them.

'Fine,' she said as the last grains of sand signalled

the power switch. 'I'll do things your way. For now,' she tagged on weakly.

The gleam in his eyes was far too dangerous to her health. She curled her fingers around her cup, willing the heat to ground her. All it did was call attention to the wave of flames rolling through her when he leaned his strong, bare forearms on the table after turning the hourglass.

'There's an event happening tonight. You will join me.'

'Considering we're joined at the hip till midnight, I don't think I have much of a choice, but okay.'

His gaze lowered for a moment, as if seeking the non-metaphorical hips she referred to. When they rose again, the gleam had intensified.

'What is the event?' she asked hurriedly to smother the feelings rampaging through her.

His lips twitched, the first genuine hint of amusement that wasn't wreathed in censure or mockery. 'I'll leave you to discover it on your own tonight, I think.'

Very few things surprised her any more so when the element of surprise became a possibility, it was always a thrill. Or was she just feeling this way because of the man delivering the surprise? 'How will I know how to get ready, then? What to wear?'

A look crossed his eyes and was gone before she could decipher it but his gaze remained as fiercely incisive. 'While you are under my roof, you need not worry that you'll lack for anything.'

There was courtesy in those words. But there was also the undeniable belief in his power and might, which was…intoxicating. And a little perturbing because Lauren would've thought she was the last person to be attracted to such raw power.

But truly, wasn't Tahir much more than that? Weren't the intriguing layers of his personality what had drawn her to him twelve years ago?

Still drew her to him now?

Watching him rise to his feet dispensed the need to examine the last question. 'Come.'

'Where are we going?'

'Does it matter? It's my time, is it not?' he said, then, catching her questioning look at the hourglass, added, 'We'll be back in time.'

She rose and fell into step beside him.

Then Tahir did the last thing she'd expected. He showed her his desert palace, trailing her through exquisite miniature orange and lemon groves, an all-white meditation room, a receiving hall made entirely of blue-veined marble, cobalt-blue pillars and a giant beaten silver fountain stunningly lit by a soaring chandelier that made her jaw drop. But her favourite room by far was the windowless library. It was lit by another grand chandelier, but all four walls held floor-to-ceiling shelves stacked with books.

'The lack of sunlight is to protect the books,' Tahir murmured, standing close to her as she spun slowly on her heel, her head thrown back to better admire the incredible space.

Drawing closer to one shelf, she read the spines of a few books and gasped. 'Some of these are… over two hundred years old.'

'My father was zealous about acquiring first-edition masterpieces. Every royal residence has such a library, but this is the largest.'

'I could spend an eternity in here,' she murmured, then her breath caught all over again when she saw the glimmer in his eyes. 'This is where you spent most of your time during your year here, isn't it?' she asked, regret tingeing her voice.

'Yes,' he responded simply. 'And before you pity me, I gained a lot of perspective during that time.'

She bit the inside of her lip. Had he gained other things too, like the hard edge she didn't remember him having twelve years ago, or had that come from ruling? And, considering most of his counterpart Arabian Peninsula monarchs and sheikhs were long married by Tahir's age, she wondered if her actions twelve years ago had contributed to his unattached status.

'Why aren't you married?' She blurted words she totally hadn't meant to ask.

He stiffened, anger flashing through his eyes before it grew cool and neutral. 'You think you had something to do with that?'

Her heart pounded hard. 'Did I?'

His lips slashed in a wide smile that didn't quite reach his eyes. 'You give yourself too much credit.'

The words stung. Deeply. But then she only had herself to blame, didn't she? Needing space, she wandered away on the pretext of admiring the rest of the library, but she could barely focus, both from the prickle of tears clouding eyes and from the fact that Tahir, having delivered that low blow, had seemingly shrugged it off, and was back to host mode, tracking her movements until she wanted to scream.

It was a relief to leave the library and step out into the fresh air on the second level. Tahir led her to an immense open terrace, drew her to the northern edge and pointed to the distance. 'That is your surprise,' he said.

Lauren stared at the horizon but all she could see were distant mountains and endless sand dunes. But squinting, she saw what he was pointing out. The faintest billowing of a cloud that hung too low to be in the sky. 'My surprise is an approaching sandstorm?' she asked, confused.

One corner of his mouth twitched. 'No, it's not a sandstorm, but it'll be here in a matter of hours,' was all he said before they were interrupted by a young staff member bearing the hourglasses.

Tahir took them and set them on the table.

As if caught in the strange time warp, they watched the grains run out, Lauren feeling as if something vital was slipping away. When the glass finally emptied, Tahir covered it again, spun the tray and watched as she made her choice again.

Forty-five minutes.

On they toured, each room in the palace more spectacular than the last, each revelation making her gasp in wonder. But the strange sensation lingered, the notion that *she* was running out of time, not Matt. That unless she acted, she would regret it.

As much as she tried to push the sensation away, it clung, growing stronger and tighter by the minute. It was still there when the servant made another appearance, murmuring to his liege in Arabic. When he left, Tahir turned to her.

'Come, our lunch is ready.'

She followed him, acutely aware that he'd never answered as to why he hadn't yet married.

Lunch was an indulgent feast, Tahir content to spend his forty-five minutes introducing her to his kingdom's delicacies, a pleasurable pastime heightened by the visual passage of time. And by the increased level of excitement within the palace as their meal grew to an end.

When it was time to choose again, Tahir's eyes gleamed with brazen satisfaction as she drew the silk from the two-and-a-half-hour hourglass. His gaze rested on the contraption for long seconds before snagging hers. 'Between us we have five hours. That is more than enough time.'

'For what?'

'To do whatever we want.' Tahir rose to his feet. 'But I suggest you return to your rooms. Your attendants are waiting for you.'

With another intense look, he left without further elaboration.

Lauren discovered the reason for the staff's excitement one hour later when she heard the growing sound of musical cries, steady drumbeats and the peculiar lyrical clicking she discovered were from finger cymbals striking in rhythm.

Standing on her terrace, she watched the large crowd edge the western plain of Tahir's villa, their voices raised in decadent, spine-tingling music as several performed jaw-dropping acrobatic moves.

'What...who are they?' she asked Nesa, who'd spent the better part of the last hour primping and styling Lauren's hair and make-up, all without giving away what it was she was getting dressed for.

The woman, who'd been courteous but slightly aloof, now gave a small smile, her gaze warming. 'They're a group of nomadic traders and performers. They always pass through when His Majesty is in residence.'

Lauren's gaze flittered over the gaily dressed crowd, her own excitement building at their carnival-like exuberance. 'How long will they stay?'

'Just one night. Which makes it even more special.'

Lauren found herself nodding, aware she was

experiencing something unique. She looked down at her own clothes.

It was another saffron-coloured outfit, but even more elaborate, with a wider band of jewelled stones etched into the neckline and the hem of the top that sat just above her belly button. The skirt was heavier too, again with rows of crystals marching down the long overlapping slits on the sides that parted to show a bit of leg when she moved.

Her shoulder burn was much better, and the light chiffon wrap protected her from the worst of the sun's rays. Her hair was caught up in an elaborate style of coiled braids and jewelled pins and she didn't need another look in the mirror to recall the understated but stunning make-up Nesa had created to make her eyes look huge and her cheekbones stand out. Somehow her favourite perfume had also been conjured up and she only needed to move a fraction to catch the scent of the fragrance.

Her gaze once more swept over the crowd and, for some unknown reason, her heart raced faster as she wondered if Tahir was down there, greeting his visitors.

'His Majesty would like you to join him downstairs,' Nesa said, as if she'd read her mind.

Several deep breaths, hallways and courtyards later, Lauren stepped into an immense, open-air receiving room. Consisting of several seating areas partly sectioned off by muslin curtains, it gave the aura of privacy while also holding a large gathering. Diamond-shaped black and white mosaic tiles drew the feet into the heart of the room while small fountains provided a soft background of serenity.

But serene was the last thing she felt as she approached the man who stood to one side of the room, his hands tucked behind his back. He was dressed from head to toe in a white kaftan, *thawb* and *keffiyeh*, the only contrasting colour the black rope holding his turban in place. With his height and breadth of shoulders, Tahir took up the whole room, commanding every scrap of her focus as his gaze latched onto her.

Lauren barely saw Nesa melt away as Tahir's eyes grew heated, gaining ferocity as they travelled over her, lingering for long moments at her neckline, the bare skin at her midriff, then finally on her glossed lips.

'My colour looks good on you,' he rasped, an indecipherable note in his voice.

Her eyes widened. 'Your colour?' Why did she sound breathless? 'You chose this colour for me?'

The barest hint of a smile twitched one corner of his mouth, then he was back to ferocious intensity again, even as one thick shoulder lifted in a shrug. 'Someone on my staff knows my favourite colour and has rightly guessed you would do it justice.'

Before she could read too much into that, he was breaching the gap between them, driving her breathless. 'You've seen the crowd outside?'

She flicked her gaze over his shoulder, towards

where the sound of revelry was steadily increasing. 'It must be nice to have your own personal carnival,' she said, attempting to tease. Anything really to lighten the atmosphere that seemed laden with…*something*.

'They're their own entity. They merely grace me with their company for a time.' Again, there was a peculiar note in his voice, his gaze lingering on hers after he spoke, enough to make further sensation tingle down her spine. 'I also know it's best to welcome them now rather than later, before things get a little…out of hand. You'll come with me.' He held out a hand in an imperious gesture that left little doubt as to his desire.

But the shock of the request stilled her. 'You want me to meet them with you?'

Something flashed in his eyes, gone far too quickly. 'Do you object to that?'

'I don't, but…' She paused, tried to reframe the jumble of words scrambled further by her wildly insane heartbeat and the intensity of the surreal feelings tumbling through her. 'Isn't it against some sort of protocol? I'm…nobody.'

This time the light arrived, burned brighter. And stayed, laser beams tearing beneath her skin, burrowing where she wasn't sure she could prevent him from landing. 'You're not nobody,' he rasped, his voice low. Intense. 'You never have been.'

Something deep, visceral, moved within her. 'Tahir.'

His nostrils flared at her uttering his name as if it moved something within him too.

Connection.

The craving throbbed hard and insistent inside her as his hand extended further, imploring and impatient at once. 'We're keeping my guests waiting. Will you join me or not?'

Any objection she had, feeble as it was, evaporated. She told herself it was because he'd couched his invitation as a question this time, that their situation demanded she stay by his side, but she knew she would've gone regardless. That unstoppable pull was binding her stronger and, try as she might, Lauren couldn't fight it. In truth, she *didn't* want to fight it any longer.

She slid her hand into his, surrendering to the wild tingles that raced up her arm as he led her to the wide doors into another courtyard and then outside where the revelling crowd cheered at the sight of their Sheikh.

Where she attempted to hide her self-consciousness as unabashed gazes swung to her and stayed, her presence by Tahir's side attracting the attention she knew it would.

Since Jukrat was a bilingual country, many of the performers responded to Tahir's introduction of her in English. She tried not to be touched by the consideration, tried...and failed not to be moved by the festive atmosphere.

An hour later, after sampling more food and

being treated to more jaw-dropping performances, she retreated to the terrace, clutching a silver goblet of wine someone had thrust into her hand at some point.

As it'd done for the better part of the evening, her gaze didn't have to roam far to land on Tahir, his words echoing in her mind.

You're not nobody. You never have been.

She knew she was a fool to personalise words she should be keeping at a distance. But then wasn't she a fool when it came to Tahir? Wasn't she, somewhere in her deepest, most secret place where her wishes wouldn't die, hoping that this pseudo fairy tale she'd found herself in would have the same ending as the one told in books?

She pressed her lips together, frantically reaching for common sense. For something solid and pragmatic to hang onto. But the combination of music, laughter and revelry, *and Tahir*, made that impossible.

'Lauren.'

She jumped, unaware he'd approached, was peering intently at her, those eyes burrowing into her secrets again.

'There's something on your mind. Tell me,' he commanded, his voice a meld of deep sensuality and concerned demand.

It was almost as if he cared.

She tried to shrug away the emotion settling on her shoulders. But the evening had been far too special to insult it with trivial dismissiveness. 'It's foolish, I know, but I don't want this—' she turned and waved her hand at the spectacle of music and dancing and exotic scents and laughter '—to end. I want to live in this moment for...' *ever*. The last word stuck in her throat because she knew even as she uttered it that her wish was as ethereal as the breeze whispering over her skin.

'There's a reason you don't want to return to your old life. Say it, Lauren,' he pressed again.

Her gaze flew to his, and locked. 'Because I don't want to go back to feeling...lost.' Whispered words that seemed to spill from deep within her soul without any prompting. But once they were said, she felt something crack within her, something she'd once thought sacred but now knew was perhaps not as treasured.

Tahir nodded, the look in his eyes reflecting deep comprehension that scared her a little. It was almost as if he'd anticipated this, as if he'd known every secret buried in her heart. 'And you won't. Because it's time to face up to it. You only felt lost because you didn't want to accept the way to your freedom. Change is hard. But it's also freeing. You've hidden yourself away for too long. Isn't it time to reach for what you truly want?'

When had he drawn so close? She could reach out, press her hand against that hard, muscled chest, feel his heartbeat...

Without conscious thought, she did just that.

His heart slammed hard against her palm, the strong, steady echo mesmeric in its rhythm. Beneath her touch, his chest expanded as he inhaled deeply. As he stood still and she touched him, the unattainable King who seemed to be in her grasp. Whose eyes swirled with the same arousal eddying through her.

'Lauren.'

There were a thousand questions in her name. But there were only a handful she wanted to answer. 'Freedom, at least for tonight, sounds good,' she said.

His heart seemed to trip, then beat just that little bit faster. Had she not placed her hand right there, she wouldn't have known her response affected him that much. But she did. And its effect was...powerful. Metaphysical. Vastly moving.

In another instinctive movement, her fingers curled, grasping a handful of his tunic to stop him from stepping away, from leaving her. They were in public, and she was all but pawing the Sheikh of Jukrat. But like everything else when it came to Tahir, it unravelled wild and untamed outside her control. As if her very soul dictated and directed her wishes before her brain could argue the toss.

A glance into his face showed her actions hadn't displeased him. He was just as unconcerned about who witnessed her bold touch.

Instead, amusement mingled with weighted

arousal and thick anticipation. Which then morphed into ferocious intent the longer she kept his gaze.

'Tell me what you want, Lauren,' he demanded hoarsely.

She knew what he was asking. It was what she'd spent every second denying from the moment she'd stepped into his office…was it only yesterday? She'd lived ten lifetimes since those tense moments.

So why not one more? It would be short, of course. But she would be in his arms. She would kiss those sensual, masterful lips. She would experience those hands on her body, his thick shaft moving inside her. All that sublime power unleashed on her.

She swayed closer, her tongue gliding out to wet her lips as desire moved like honey through her veins.

He made a sound in his throat, a cross between frustration and warning. The hand imprisoning hers on his chest squeezed, a firm insistence that she answer.

'I want the freedom…to be with you.'

To find myself with you the way I did twelve years ago.

CHAPTER EIGHT

SHE DIDN'T SAY those words out loud, of course. She was many things, but she wasn't a fool, and the last thing she wanted was to throw the anvil of that reminder between them. Not now. Not when he'd steered her into believing she could be something different. Something more.

That the kernel of *something* she'd refused to nurture because it resembled betrayal wasn't that at all. It'd been self-preservation. A compass that had refused to stay hidden because it was vital to who she was meant to be. Tahir had forced her to dig it free. To dust it off and dare to look at where it pointed.

He'd given her that.

And if he wanted her as much as she wanted him…wasn't that just the icing on the cake?

'Take me to bed, Tahir,' she breathed, every emotion she'd felt for this man shaking through her. 'I want you,' she added, just so there was no confusion.

She gasped when he immediately wrapped one muscled arm around her, pulled her close to plaster her to his body.

No, the Sheikh of Jukrat didn't care who witnessed his heated interaction with her.

Why that thrilled her from the roots of her hair to her very toes, she was thankfully saved from exploring when he lowered his head and sealed her mouth with his. His tongue swept inside, stroking hers with slow, firm glides that tunnelled desire straight between her legs. Even before she released his tunic to wind both hands around his neck, her panties were damp, her clitoris swollen and needy, her arousal a tsunami already threatening to sweep her away.

Lauren barely felt him move her backward, didn't care where he was taking her. The cool touch of a solid wall behind her was immediately ameliorated by the hard, living flame of Tahir's body caging hers.

He feasted on her with animalistic intensity and relish, raw sounds rasping from his throat as he plundered her mouth. His fingers drove into her hair, firm fingers angling her head for better access.

And she gave it to him. Gave her all to the searing kiss that felt as vital as breathing, the fire of it sweeping through her, branding her.

One hand dropped to claim her hip, to drag her even closer so she couldn't mistake the force of his arousal against her belly. Lauren moaned, need building until she believed she would combust.

But then, Tahir moved again, lifting his head to place a little distance between them. Fevered eyes raked her face, lingering on her swollen mouth before he exhaled audibly.

'As much as I want to take you right here, right now, I don't think my people are ready to be scandalised by their Sheikh in such a manner, do you?' he rasped.

'Won't they mind you leaving them?' she asked, even though she was more than willing to be done with the celebration.

'They've had more than enough of me. Now it's your turn.'

The intent and promise in his voice melted her from the inside out, the thought of wasting any more time dragging a frustrated moan to her throat. Luckily, she managed to swallow it back down, but Tahir's nostrils flared nonetheless at whatever he read in her face.

'You would drag a man to his doom, *habibti*,' he declared thickly.

'Then it's a good thing you're not just any man, isn't it?' She didn't know where she found the wherewithal to tease but greedy flames of excitement lit through her when he gave a helpless groan.

His fingers encircled her wrist, dragging her from the wall. Guards and servants bowed and stepped back as he strode through the villa.

Expecting him to use the main courtyards and hallways, she was surprised when he headed for the far end of the eastern wing.

The sound of music and laughter faded as he

stopped beside an inner wall covered by a towering vine in the farthest courtyard. Despite the few lit lamps, she didn't see exactly what he did, but she gasped when a section of the wall gave way to reveal a long, semi-lit passage.

'What…where are we?' she asked. Her voice shook, not because she was afraid, but because this was far too much like the fairy tales she'd discarded decades ago but, it seemed, still lived somewhere in her heart.

In the semidarkness, she caught the wicked flash of his eyes as he looked down at her. 'When my great-grandfather built this villa, he incorporated a few… interesting designs.'

'Like secret passages?'

His lips curved, his teeth flashing as he smiled. 'Among other things.'

They walked for a full minute, bypassing a handful of entrances before he stopped at one. When he pressed on another discreet panel, it sprang open to reveal a long, familiar-looking hallway.

'Is that…are we near my room?'

'Yes. Your suite connects to mine, and we share this wing,' he said, as if it was the most natural thing in the world. And perhaps in his world such a thing was natural. In truth, she'd discovered so many different things after less than twenty-four hours in Tahir's orbit that demonstrated just how much she'd kept a shroud over herself.

And…she was eager to embrace it all.

When he lengthened his strides, she fell in beside him. And when he nudged the imposing door open and stepped into his suite, she girded her loins and stepped into the experience.

Tahir's suite was unashamedly masculine, the bold terracotta colour scheme broken only by thin accents of gold. But interspersed with it were the usual splashes of equally bold colour she was beginning to associate with all things Jukrati.

Brocade sofas were positioned in the vast room with exquisite paintings and indigenous tapestries gracing the walls. But it was the emperor-sized bed that held her attention.

It was a work of art.

It was erected on an immense raised platform, the headboard a magnificent creation of dark ebony petrified wood, carved and polished into a masterpiece she would've loved to study, had Tahir's hand not trailed up her arm and shoulder to clench in her hair, his other arm banding her waist once more. A shudder rushed through her at the passionate hold, her body blindly pivoting into his as he angled her head for another dominating kiss.

They kissed until she was breathless. Until she firmly believed she would climax from the magic of it alone. Her head was still spinning, her senses screaming when he broke the kiss and whirled her around.

He drew her hair back from her neck and trailed kisses down her spine, his hands wreaking equally delightful devastation. When his hands framed her hips, she turned to watch him.

The sight of Tahir on his haunches behind her, his gaze searing every inch of skin it touched, was enough to make her sway on her feet. One hand reached out to steady her, then, the moment she stilled, he tracked the backs of his hands up her legs, slowly, in an unhurried exploration that had her panting in under a minute.

'Your skin is like the warmest silk.' He reached the curve beneath her bottom and stroked the line from the outside in, pausing just before where she was hot and damp and almost embarrassingly needy. His nostrils flared and Lauren watched him visibly swallow. 'And you smell intoxicating.'

Firmly, he nudged her legs apart, the thumbs stroking her inner thighs skating tantalisingly close to her apex. When his lips parted hungrily, she gave a needful moan, breaths shuddering out of her as her need built and built.

'Do you want me to pleasure you? Taste this beautiful gift you're offering?'

The tremor coursing through her turned her nipples to hard points and there wasn't a single cell in her body that didn't screech *yes* to his husky query. 'Please, Tahir. I need you.'

His whole body seemed to surge at her response, an animalistic growl leaving his throat as he gripped her thighs harder, held her captive as he rolled forward onto his knees. And delivered on his promise.

Her eyes clamped shut, pleasure overflowing. It felt like the most natural thing in the world, to reach back, spear her fingers through his hair and hold him to his task. And from the healthy grunt he gave, he more than approved her enthusiasm.

Thick curses left his throat as he lapped at her, the expert swirls of his tongue at her core and over her clitoris driving her deeper into insanity until, with a cry torn from her throat, Lauren exploded in a heady climax.

She struggled to catch her breath as stars darted and tumbled behind her eyelids, as she felt him surge to his feet, a firm hand at her back to tumble her into bed.

When she finally dragged her eyelids open, it was to the sexiest striptease from the Sheikh of Jukrat, his eyes latching onto hers as he slowly stripped.

Once naked, he prowled onto the bed to crouch over her, and Lauren truly believed he was the most spectacular sight she'd ever seen.

And because it'd been so long, because she'd yearned for him so, she shamelessly explored him. From his taut cheekbones to the square jaw clenched tight to control his arousal, to the glorious landscape of collarbone, chiselled pecs and sculptured abs, he was a living, breathing tapestry of masculinity she wanted to revel in until time stopped.

Need built again, demanding satisfaction. So when, with a growl, he captured her hands and pinned them above her head on the bed, his eyes staring intently into her eyes for a minute before he swooped down to capture her mouth again, she let him, swopping one heady experience for another with an eagerness that mildly alarmed her. And then that too was washed away, obliterated by the body pressing down onto hers, the wicked tongue that had just made her come so spectacularly stroking hers, ratcheting up the fever in her veins.

They kissed until her lips burned with passion, until her legs were wrapped tight around him, her body molten and ready.

With almost driven purpose, he tore his lips away to stare down at her once more, savage desire etched into his face. 'You wreck my control so effortlessly,' he charged, then he shook his head. 'I should be immune to you. Should be done with this fever you invoke in my blood,' he finished with a hoarse growl. But even as he spoke, one hand was moving over her body, capturing her breast and moulding it, his nostrils flaring as he toyed with her nipple.

'But you're not,' she dared to counter, feminine power weaving through her with an intoxication she could see becoming addictive, very quickly. But then, she didn't need to worry about that, did she? In a handful of hours, this would be over. Whether she succeeded or failed, her life was back in England.

With her family…

That punch of rejection struck again. The arrow-sharp hunch that, whatever happened here, she wouldn't return home the same. That the Lauren she'd been when she boarded the plane a handful of days ago had irreparably changed.

'Lauren.'

The snap of her name drew her from her morose thoughts.

'I am the only one you will think about,' he decreed with an arrogance that should've annoyed her. But how could it when she wholeheartedly wished the same? When she didn't want to think about what tomorrow held for her?

'Yes. Only you,' she breathed.

His eyes flared with satisfaction, then darkened dramatically as she rolled her hips against the power of his erection that throbbed insistently between her legs.

'Tahir.' His name was like the finest wine, full-bodied and languorously savoured, the extra pleasure of it the look on his face as she said it.

A shudder raked through him.

Then he was moving, tugging open a hidden compartment on the side of the bed she hadn't even noticed. He reared onto his knees and tore open the packaging on the condom he'd retrieved. Jaw clenched hard once more, he rolled it on.

She started to draw down her arms, to reach for him, to caress the hard rod of his manhood. But he recaptured her hand, holding her effortlessly with one as the other clutched her hip.

'Enough, *habibti*. You can explore to your heart's content later. Right now, I must have you…need to be inside you,' he said with a jagged gruffness that transmitted straight to her blood. The thought that he was far gone for her was a heady thing indeed.

But, as she knew he would, he claimed his power back, delivering a searing kiss before, positioning himself at her heated core, Tahir drove slowly and relentlessly inside her.

Her moan was deep and long and soul-shaking, the pleasure of his possession shaking the foundations of her being. 'Oh, God!'

He stilled; his eyes molten as he stared down at her. 'So tight. You feel…' He shook his head once more. 'How long since you took a lover?' he rasped tightly.

Heat rushed up into her face, her eyes widening. 'What?'

Kisses trailed from the corner of her mouth to the shell of her ear. 'Your delicious snugness tells a story.'

As if to relay how much he relished that story, he moved, rolling his hips in a sublime undulation that had her whole body surging in appreciation.

'How long?' he pressed when all she did was try to hang on.

'Tahir…' She paused, knowing he wouldn't let this go. 'A few years…' she managed to slur.

Triumph blazed in the eyes that met hers, as if her celibacy was a trophy he'd won. And perhaps it was. After all, hadn't the very rare sex she'd indulged in after Tahir been a perfunctory act, even a last-ditch means to find connection that never materialised?

'Is your ego adequately stroked, Your Majesty?' she murmured, then, with a wicked urge to retain some ground, she rolled her own hips.

An unguarded groan left his throat, his breathing turning agitated. Then as if a switch had been flicked, his grip on her hip tightened, his strokes gaining a rapid and relentless rhythm that had her tossing her head in lust-filled abandon.

'Yes! Oh, yes,' she cried. Her throaty pleas seemed to trigger him into faster movement. His possession grew frenzied, his eyes as wild and untamed as his beloved desert.

Long after sweat had slicked both their skins and her throat had grown hoarse, he was drawing further demands of her body. And she granted each one, tumbling from one release to the other until, with a guttural roar, Tahir finally achieved his own.

CHAPTER NINE

TAHIR DIDN'T FIGHT the sublime sensation stealing through his veins. But as their bodies cooled and a drowsy Lauren drifted off into sleep in his arms, he braced himself for the storm of emotions and questions rushing at him.

Curiously, regret stayed muted in the background, a mirage content to keep its distance. He didn't mind. He didn't regret what had just happened. What troubled him most was the seeming… *inevitability* of the whole thing.

Somehow, he'd known in his bones in those moments after she'd blurted out her plea on his helipad that they would end up here, in this position, their limbs tangled around each other in post-coital abandon. Were he the type to believe in the cosmic, he'd think this was written in the stars. That true control wasn't his when it came to Lauren Winchester.

But he wasn't such a type. He'd suspected this might happen. He'd resisted but, ultimately, he'd been unable to stop it. Because he hadn't wanted to, despite all signs pointing to it being a bad idea?

He clenched his jaw, fighting the implication that he was so weak-willed when it came to this woman. But wasn't he? He'd barely managed twenty-four hours before succumbing to her allure. They'd fallen into bed while the serious issues of her remorse and his forgiveness remained in the balance. Hell, he'd devolved into playing *tour guide*, showing off the very place she'd had him banished to, then compounded it all by inviting her to greet his guests at his side.

He hadn't even spared more than a fleeting thought for the rampant speculation he would be inviting by that last action.

All because he'd yearned to see her come alive and would've done anything to achieve it?

He exhaled, attempting to escape the discomfort of his own thoughts. He knew before morning his advisors would be demanding to know the same thing—what had he been thinking? But they wouldn't stop there.

They would probe and nuance-seek his actions to death. Or until they were satisfied it wasn't a harbinger of some other decision.

He shifted, his mind attempting to sidestep the unfeasible thought that wanted to sprout. Except that task, too, seemed impossible. Come midnight, questions would come. For answers he didn't have.

Or did he?

Discomfort warred with anticipation, producing a disconcerting mix.

Against him, Lauren moved, sighed and curled her hand over his chest.

He needed to get up, vacate the room or move her to her own bed.

But…his gaze tracked across the room to the hourglass his valet had delivered here hours ago at his direction. They were still caught up in the game, weren't they?

And which part of the game is this?

The part where he abandoned everything his grandfather had taught him for the sake of a woman? The part where he could hear his own father's condemnation even from the beyond?

He gritted his teeth tighter. Wasn't he above that, though? His father had had his own flaws. He'd been too strict. Too set in his ways to bend and move with the times. To bend and move for his children. His marriage had barely survived what he himself had preached.

Wasn't Tahir entitled to his own opinions? His own path? His own mistakes?

Plural?

Disconcertion grew. Wasn't one mistake with this woman enough?

Or was he being disingenuous? Now he knew more about the circumstances of her past, could *he* find it in himself to bend a little, the way his own father hadn't quite been able to?

The voice echoing a response within him was far too strong. Far too definitive.

But he couldn't rush into decision. Didn't he owe himself the right to be a little circumspect? Or was he pushing for time on a situation he'd already decided on?

He tried to tune out the voice mocking him that he'd already forgiven her completely and was playing for time. That he was reaching for circumspection far too late. He'd thoroughly spent himself with Lauren, given in to incandescent passion that still seared the edges of his senses.

Passion he wanted to relive all over again. And again.

It was that all-consuming need that finally drove him from the bed and past the hourglass that was slowly dwindling the last of Lauren's time. Time she'd given up to be with him. He shook his head, unwilling to read more into it.

And yet he couldn't prise his gaze from the whispering falls of sand, from the sensations moving within him, urging him to seize this moment before it passed.

Before it was too late…

His gaze drifted back to the woman laid out on his bed. Need punched through him one more time, and he had to lock his knees to stop himself from stalking back to the bed, waking her…

No.

Sex was addling his brain. Throwing on a dressing gown, he stepped out onto the terrace, choosing to let Lauren sleep.

Hell, he welcomed it to sort through his own thoughts. The sun had gone down, and his nomadic guests would be readying to leave so they could arrive at another oasis before midday tomorrow.

For a single moment, he envied their freedom. To do as they wished. No greater responsibility than fulfilling their next desires. With whomever they chose. Without consequence or duty or politics dictating their actions.

He…yearned for that.

Forgive her, and you can have it…

The voice whispered on a breeze, ruffling his hair and further unsettling his emotions. Was it a lack of sleep directing his thoughts this way?

A sharp intake of breath brought all his thoughts crashing to a halt.

But he didn't turn around. Because in that moment, Tahir knew the thing he yearned for the most was the woman rousing from his bed. The woman he sensed coming closer.

Her scent, mingled with the sweat and sex they'd heartily indulged in, reached his nostrils before she did. He attempted to brace himself but that infernal emotion punched through him again when she slid her body…her *near naked* body, against his.

'I didn't mean to fall asleep,' she murmured, her voice sleep-husky, sexy and far too alluring to be borne with the types of thoughts he was having.

'It was your time to do with as you wished.'

He felt her stiffen ever so slightly and felt a tinge of regret for dragging up the reason for their game.

The culmination of which he was still unsure how to deal with.

He pushed that thought out of his mind for the moment, and, because he seemed incapable of resisting her, he wrapped his arm around her waist and tugged her between him and the stone balustrade of his terrace. Then almost wished he hadn't when a quick glance down confirmed she was draped in nothing but the saffron silk wrap she'd worn over her attire this evening.

Instantly, he felt his body rise, his blood thrumming quicker through his veins.

'The sand ran out a minute ago. I turned it so it's your time now,' she murmured, her far too tempting lips so close. So sumptuous.

'Then I have in mind exactly what I wish to do.'

He scooped her up, revelling in her gasp and the way her arms instantly curled around his neck.

Addictive.

Obsessive.

Dangerous.

All words that pounded through his brain, attempting to pull the brakes on something he suspected was already too late as he strode in sure steps past secret, darkened hallways and courtyards to another treasured destination.

There, he listened to her gasp again, watched pleasure unfurl on her face as she glanced around her.

'Where are we?'

'My private bath chamber.'

Her eyes widened. 'Another one?'

'No one uses this one but me.'

He let her body slide down his until her feet dropped next to his. Then he was sliding his fingers into her hair, capturing her nape and dragging her closer.

'I haven't had nearly enough of you,' he grunted, the confession torn from his soul.

Her green eyes latched onto his and he could've fooled himself that he saw adoration in there. Perhaps even the same yearning that swelled like a billowing sandstorm through him.

He convinced himself it was a trick of the light as he lowered his head. As he took her lips, felt hers cling to him and tried to swat away the emotions battering away at him.

This was nothing more than sex.

Two and a half hours. He would use all of it. Indulge to his body's content.

Then he would get back on track.

His infernal yearning *would* be contained.

Her throat was raw from screaming in ecstasy. The moment Tahir had assured her they were entirely private and wouldn't be either heard or disturbed, Lauren felt as if a passion tap had been turned onto full.

Except she was beginning to suspect it wasn't merely passion. Passion wouldn't have triggered the sort of panic she'd felt when she'd woken alone, afraid she'd frittered her precious time with Tahir away with sleep.

Her precious time?

Yes, those three words had been equally terrifying. Because again, Matt had failed to feature in her thoughts, and, worse still, her guilt had been minimal.

She had been thinking entirely of herself. Of the hairline cracks in her heart she suspected had occurred a very long time ago. Twelve years, in fact, when she'd walked away from Tahir Al-Jukrat. Cracks that had grown wider with each moment spent in his presence, leaking emotions she feared she couldn't contain for much longer.

'Am I losing you?'

Thick words that dragged her attention back to the present. To the man stretched out beside her on the blanket beneath the stars, one hand on her hip while the other fondled her breast.

Dear heaven, but he was magnificent. Despite the sun having set, there was enough light to make out the chiselled perfection of his features.

No, but I lost you.

She swallowed, for a split second terrified she'd spoken the words aloud. But the quizzical, watchful look in his eyes said he was awaiting an answer.

'I'm right here,' she said, attempting lightness she didn't feel.

The look in his eyes didn't change. 'Are you?'

he mused, the tiniest hint of an edge in his voice. 'I find myself in the peculiar circumstance of wanting to know what a woman is thinking.'

Panic flared higher. She couldn't tell him her true feelings, of course. That would be like baring her jugular to a predator. 'I'm thinking that I have a question I'd like to ask.'

One corner of his mouth lifted, amusement mingling with languid satiation on his face. A part of her felt awe for reducing the supreme ruler of Jukrat to a satisfied, post-sex haze. But the greater part of her was still caught in alarm at the passing of time. At the heavier weight of her emotions with each passing second. At the keen knowledge that their twenty-four hours would end with having changed on a fundamental level.

'I'm not entirely sure how to take asking permission before asking.'

She hadn't consciously framed the question. It seemed dragged out of her soul, perhaps a puzzle piece she wanted in place for herself. 'Did you ever manage to repair your relationship with your father?'

His touch tightened on her flesh for a short second before he released her. Jaw clenched, he rolled away from her. 'That is not a subject I like to discuss in bed.'

'Technically, we're not in bed,' she teased, desperate to reverse time. Wishing she didn't feel a chill in her soul when he was still within touching distance. But with every avenue seemingly paved with emotional landmines, she was stuck.

'Ah, I'm afraid the cushion of technicalities won't make me any more amenable.' Shoulders stiff, he rose from the blanket and prowled into the semi-darkened space. A second later, he was shrugging on a robe that seemed to have materialised out of nowhere but was probably tucked into all the discreet, magical corners his tents and desert residences contained.

Without speaking further, he padded to one of the giant boulders surrounding the bathing area, his gaze still averted from her. And for several minutes, a grim silence cocooned them.

'Now it's my turn to ask whether I've lost you.' Her voice was soft. Shaky. Its meaning far deeper than the obvious.

You never had him. He was a previous but temporary gift you foolishly squandered.

Feeling far too naked on the blanket, she rose too, slipped the wrap over her shoulders before folding her arms around her waist. She looked up to find his eyes fixed on her. Mild displeasure warred with something else. Yearning, possibly. Or at least a window beyond which something glinted, like a… *proffer.*

She stopped herself from reaching out, grasping it with both hands. Like everything beautiful and magical in this time and space, it was transient. A mirage.

And yet, she remained…hopeful as he exhaled. 'I've mentioned more than once that I'm not the man you used to know.'

Her heart lurched painfully, then dropped.

But he was continuing. 'My time in the desert forged that change.' His lips twisted. 'For starters, I didn't trust a single word the print media said about anything from then onwards.' His face resettled into austere lines. 'But to answer your question, yes, I became more of the man my father wanted me to be.'

'And what was that?'

'Steeped in duty to the Jukrati people. Rebuilding the reputation of my beloved kingdom. In the end, I gained his approval.'

The words were as austere as his expression, a literal answer to a literal question. She licked her lips, fighting the urge to let it be. But she couldn't. Because, right along with everything she'd wanted for this man, she wanted him to have found peace with his father, too. 'Did he ever forgive you?'

A bleakness fleetingly shrouded his face, gone the next instant. 'I didn't ask for forgiveness, and he never indicated I would get it. But according to those in his council, he died believing I would rule Jukrat ably enough.'

'And your mother?'

His expression grew tighter. 'What about her?'

'You explained the relationship you have. But… did you ever ask her why she signed the document?'

He frowned. 'There is no excuse for agreeing to such a thing.'

'Even in arranged marriages, especially if perhaps some council of advisors suggest it?'

His expression darkened further, but just as before he seemed disarmed, as if the possibility hadn't occurred to him. Then he shook his head. 'Why are we discussing this?'

She shrugged. 'You've given your opinion, repeatedly, about my family situation. I thought it only fair to return the favour.'

'But unlike you, I've accepted the glaring truth. And moved on with my life.'

Heart caught in a tighter vice, and not wanting him to see how much she hurt for him, she dropped her gaze.

'You don't look content with my response, Lauren,' he said after a full minute.

Confused and, yes, a little desperate at how much his happiness meant to her, she let out a shaky laugh. 'Content? How can anyone be content by a father not telling his son that he's proud of him? That he loves him? And a mother who might feel more but is unable to show it?'

He exhaled harshly, the corners of his lips pinched tight. 'Perhaps because neither of them deemed me worthy.'

'That's absurd!'

He stiffened, those eyes burnishing brighter.

Sharper. Drilling straight into her vulnerable spaces. 'Why?'

'Because…' She froze too, her heart caught in her throat.

Because you deserve love. You deserve to be loved the way I love you.

The truth shook her to her last cell. And it came with laughable inevitability.

Of course she loved him.

She'd loved him for twelve long, lonely years when she'd lived less than a half-life.

'Because?' he demanded tightly.

She cleared her throat of the rock of truth waiting to tumble free. 'Because every child deserves to be told they're loved, no matter what.'

The light dimmed, a harder tension seizing his body. 'Surely you know by now that receiving what one deserves is often not a foregone conclusion. If it helps, I didn't think my time here was a total disaster.'

Registering that she was clinging to straws didn't stop her from pushing. 'So *you* believe that something good came of it?'

A fierce light illuminated his eyes, turning them golden in the lamplight. 'Until recently, I imagined so,' he rasped, his lips barely moving. 'But I've changed my mind.'

A chill swept into her heart. Because she realised then her questioning had another agenda. She'd been gearing up to ask if *he* forgave her. Whether they could, at the very least, part without acrimony.

If nothing good came of his time here, then he still believed she'd taken that time from him. He'd lost a year with his grandfather because of her.

Hot tears prickled her eyes, a tumult of emotion building and building until she feared everything would come tumbling out.

But…perhaps that wasn't a bad thing? So much had happened between yesterday and today. Dared she plead her case one more time?

Before she could chicken out, she rose from the blanket. 'Tahir, I'm sorry.'

He frowned, then jerked upright from where he'd leaned against the boulder. 'You misunderstand what I meant, Lauren. I've changed my mind because there's nothing to—' He paused as footsteps approached.

When a disembodied voice spoke in low, urgent tones, Tahir frowned and answered.

Lauren wanted to shout at the intruder to go away. She needed to hear what he'd been about to say.

But striding forward, Tahir picked up a silk wrap, again conjured seemingly out of nowhere, and gently draped it over her shoulders. For a taut few seconds, he simply stared at her, questions teeming in his eyes. But she recognised the moment he shut them down.

'I'm needed on an urgent call. But this conversation isn't over. We'll pick it up when I'm done, yes?'

Even more bewildered, she nodded jerkily, her heart leaping wildly in her chest as he tugged her close and brushed a soft kiss on her forehead.

Then he was striding away, his magnificent towering figure disappearing before she took her next breath.

He must've given instructions regarding her because, a handful of minutes later, Nesa and another attendant appeared, and she was ushered back to her suite.

Thankfully, they left her when she insisted she could dress herself.

After rinsing off and donning fresh clothes, hair brushed and the lightest make-up applied more for fortitude than anything else, she was about to head out onto her terrace for some much-needed head-clearing air when she recalled that the hourglasses were in Tahir's suite.

She debated leaving them alone, but it seemed essential that they finished what they'd started.

She was now familiar enough with the hallways on this level to navigate her way to his private quarters. Expecting a hovering aide or attendant who would let her in to retrieve the hourglasses, Lauren was surprised when she found the hallways empty.

Approaching Tahir's doors, she tentatively knocked. To no response.

Biting her lip, she turned the handle and entered.

The first time she'd entered these quarters, it'd been through the secret passage. When she'd left it, she'd been far too distracted to see which way Tahir took. Now, she saw that within the quarters were three smaller hallways, each shooting off into more rooms. She bypassed an elaborate sunken living area and went down a corridor that turned out to be guest bedroom before retracing her steps. The second led to an immense kitchen and sleek gym.

The third revealed the master suite she sought.

Heat billowed inside her as she took in the rumpled sheets and discarded clothes. The half-finished bottle of wine Tahir had opened after they'd made love the first time stood on his bedside table.

She turned a full circle in the room, desperately etching every corner of it in her brain so she could draw on it when the future grew too bleak.

When her gaze landed on the hourglass on top of a hand-carved cabinet, her eyes widened. Had they really only been gone just over an hour? She went towards the tray, her heart hammering with each step.

After this she would only have a turn or two before midnight struck. Three if she was lucky. She would continue to advocate for Matt, of course.

But didn't she matter, too?

She was *still* in love with Tahir.

Did she not owe it to herself to fight her own corner? Her own happiness? To lay all her cards on the table?

What if he rejects you?

Her fingers trembled against the filigree casing of the hourglass. But she raised her chin. She'd just been reminded, *by Tahir*, that she had hidden strength. Wouldn't it see her through?

The rejection of her parents was one thing, but the rejection of the man she loved…? The man who was everything her heart and soul desired? Could she withstand it if her hopes were dashed?

She clenched her fist, the answer too terrible to contemplate. And yet…

Could she live with herself if she didn't?

No, she couldn't.

A strange, almost euphoric resolve in place, Lauren whirled about. Then stopped. Tahir was occupied with a phone call elsewhere. Should she wait for him here or return to her room?

Here.

Decision made, she stepped out onto the terrace because being in the room where he'd made such sublime love to her threatened to scramble her brain. For what lay ahead, she needed every available faculty.

Night-time in the desert was even more mesmerising than the day. The elements of danger that lingered only heightened the brightness of the start, the crispness of the air. Eyes on the constellation, she gasped softly when a comet streaked across the sky.

She wasn't too far gone to make a wish, but she

hoped with every fibre of her being that this time he wouldn't slip through her fingers too soon.

That she would be—

Tahir's deep, serious tones interrupted her fanciful thoughts, for which she was half grateful. Pulse racing, she turned, but he wasn't in the bedroom or on the terrace with her. It dawned on her that the labyrinthine layout of the villa meant he could be above, below or in a room beside her.

It turned out he was on a half-level above her, on a smaller terrace connecting to what looked like a study.

The last thing Lauren wanted was to be caught eavesdropping on a conference call.

And she would've retreated from the terrace had she not heard her name uttered by a voice she didn't recognise.

Her feet froze. Her palms grew clammy. Every instinct urged her to leave. But Tahir was responding. And with the resonance of a sonic boom, shattered every last one of her dreams.

'You've wasted both your time and mine by gambling with a weak hand, Adnan. Lauren Winchester has no bearing on the decisions I make regarding my kingdom, at present or in the future. If you think I'm distracted enough by her or you are spying on me to see what happens with her brother so you can leverage it to alter a single clause in our agreement, you're going to be woefully disappointed. Nothing has changed. Nothing

will change. Javid has agreed to help you advance
this agreement. I suggest you make the most of
his expertise. That is the only concession you will
receive.'

CHAPTER TEN

Iṭ DIDN'T TAKE Tahir very long at all to realise he'd taken this call for one reason only. Distance.

An excuse to step back from the emotions bombarding him when Lauren dragged up painful subjects. So fast on the heels of his own soul-searching, he'd felt as if he were coming apart at the seams.

He'd taken the reprieve. And now every cell in his body was straining to be back there with her. To jump into the deep end and to hell with keeping his every emotion locked down tight.

In a world where everyone wanted something from him—case in point, this conversation with his cousin—Lauren had asked for nothing for herself except his forgiveness. Forgiveness she still believed he withheld because he hadn't fully conveyed it before they'd been interrupted.

He frowned, impatience digging deeper claws into him as his cousin droned on.

As he'd suspected, Adnan had played the card he believed would sway Tahir. Now he was tugging on family bonds, with mild threats thrown in about knowledge of Winchester's arrest. Tahir heard Javid's faint snort in the background. He would've laughed himself had the need to get back to Lauren not been so visceral. If this was what twenty minutes away from her felt like, how would it be when their twenty-four *hours* were up?

What would it be like if she left him…?

'…for the sake of my future heirs,' Adnan petitioned plaintively.

Future…heirs.

Tahir jack-knifed in his chair, sending an expensive paperweight skidding across his desk. Tense silence echoed from the connection, then, 'Everything all right?' his cousin asked.

Control honed since birth came to his aid as, with his heart jammed firmly in his throat, he answered evenly, 'I'm not interested in going around in circles with you, cousin. This conversation is over.'

He hung up and jumped to his feet, his urgent strides eating up the distance to his private suite. Tahir wasn't sure why he'd assumed she would be there and the tingling sensation at the back of his neck didn't help as he barked at an aide as to her whereabouts.

Miss Winchester had returned to her rooms and taken the hourglasses with her, he was told.

He found her on her terrace, seated on a trellised chair with refreshments set out. Refreshments she hadn't touched.

Was it his imagination or did her back stiffen as he approached? He couldn't quite tell in the lamplight. Cool eyes drifted his way and a small smile played at her lips.

He wanted to sweep her into his arms, kiss those lips until they clung to his. Until she was mad with the same turbulent emotions coursing through him. But he needed a level head. Too much hinged on this new, intensely unnerving turn of events.

'Ah, there you are. I brought these in here so we don't lose track of the game. I hope you don't mind.'

Tahir frowned. There was a chilled civility in her tone he'd never heard before. He'd heard her fired up about solutions to a humanitarian crisis, heard her passionate, disconsolate, and defiant. But never these snooty cut-glass upper-class tones her brother and his cronies favoured.

Giving his head a silent shake, he strode closer, the subject throbbing wildly inside him driving his every breath. 'We need to talk.'

She waved a graceful hand at the hourglass. 'Of course. It's still your allotted time. Fire away.'

Since there was no delicate way to approach this, and because, hell, he didn't want to, he stated bluntly, 'I didn't use protection the last time. Is there a possibility that I've made you pregnant?'

Lauren felt the blood drain from her face. Of all the ways she'd imagined their next conversation going after what she'd overheard, this was the last thing she'd expected.

The hand next to her untouched glass of sweet tea trembled wildly and she was absurdly glad she hadn't picked it up to take a sip. Because she was sure she'd have shattered—

'Lauren?' he pressed. His face might have been a mask of rigid control, but electric tension vibrated from him. And his eyes...if they'd been burnished gold before, they were the colour of flaming sand now. Alive and all-consuming.

It isn't for you. It's for the situation he finds himself in. Another scandal...

The reminder was bracing enough to restore a modicum of calm. 'And what if I'm pregnant? Are you going to strike a bargain with me too the way your mother did with your father and with you?' She flinched the moment the words left her lips. Then she cursed herself for her soft heart.

For a single moment, he looked incandescent. Then his ashen features neutralised. 'Is that what you want?'

'No!'

At her forceful answer a touch of tension eased in his tight shoulders. But the majority of it remained. 'Tell me what you want.'

An hour ago, she would've cried with joy to hear those words. 'And you'll grant it? Why don't I believe that?'

His hands slid into his pockets. 'You won't know until you state it.'

'Fine. It's easy enough. I want to finish this game and return home.'

A tic throbbed at his temple. Then, 'No.'

Don't panic. 'No? Just like that? You know you can't hold me prisoner, right?'

He sauntered away and leaned against the terrace wall as if he had all the time in the world. 'I won't need to. Before we're done talking, you'll be agreeable to what I have in mind.'

'You sound very sure of yourself.'

'I've had practice,' he said without an ounce of self-doubt.

'This isn't some sort of business transaction.' The words seared her throat, her every emotion turning her insides raw.

He inclined his head. 'No, it's very personal. But it's a transaction nonetheless.'

'A transaction you think you'll win.'

'We'll both win.'

She tilted her head, dying to unsettle him as much as his calm assuredness was unsettling her. 'And how do you work that out?'

'Because I will make you my queen.'

He tossed the words out as if he were announcing what his palace chef was cooking for dinner.

Her jaw sagged to the floor and for the life of her she couldn't pick it back up because a multitude of emotions held her captive. When she managed to speak it was to eject one stunned word. 'What?'

'You're not deaf, Lauren.'

Her gaze flicked above his head, to the stars she'd stood under such a short time ago and stopped herself from making fruitless wishes. It seemed the cosmos had taken it upon itself to deliver a poisoned wish nonetheless. Because what could be more devastating than being granted a lifetime beside the love of your life when he was doing it out of duty?

'No, I'm not. Which makes me wonder if you're the one who's gone insane.'

His whole body bristled with affront, his eyes narrowing into laser missiles. 'Excuse me?'

'You're not deaf, Tahir.' She launched his words back at him, the voice screeching at her to watch her tone conclusively ignored.

'You question whether I'm impaired because I want to keep my child and heir under my roof and my protection?'

'No, I question your reasoning as to why you think you need to do that by marrying a woman you don't want. A woman who doesn't want you back.' She tagged on because it felt vital that she clarify that lest he believe otherwise.

It was clear that clarification was over-exaggerated when his gaze tunnelled into hers, his expression patently mocking. 'You don't want me? Really? Shall I prove to you how much you don't want me?'

'Isn't that how we found ourselves here in the first place? Trying to prove some sort of point to each other?'

'I'm happy to give you a lasting refresher that would make you stop lying to yourself once and for all,' he proffered, the eyes boring into hers absolutely deadly with intent.

'No, thanks.' Her voice was prim, but her emotions were anything but.

Challenge flared in his eyes for a moment, ramping up every cell in her body in response. Then, like the imperious ruler he was, confident in his power and influence, he bared his teeth in a smile.

'Then shall we get back to the discussion?'

'I've said all I'm going to say.'

He folded his arms, and she categorically forbade her gaze from dropping to his brawny forearms. Arms she'd gripped as she'd drowned in the pleasure he'd created. Of course, her senses had other ideas.

They prompted her gaze to seek out the gap opening at the throat of his tunic, to feast on the swathe of bronze skin displayed there, then up to gorge on the lines of his strong throat. When it then travelled up to meet his, the far too knowing and abashedly carnal look he returned flared heat into her cheeks.

'Let me get this straight. You intend to return to England, where you'll give birth to my child and live with them under your parents' roof with no argument from me?'

The desert-dry incredulity in his voice made her flinch. Because, set out like that, it was as unlikely as sprouting wings and flying away from this increasingly terrifying conversation.

'All this is highly hypothetical. We don't even

know if I'm pregnant,' she said, cringing at the touch of desperation in her voice.

He didn't budge from where he stood. Nor did he lessen the laser focus of his gaze. And Lauren should've hated the under-the-microscope sensation that triggered, but unnervingly being such intense focus of Tahir's gaze was…thrilling. And desperately heartbreaking.

'You didn't just have sex with a guy you met on a dating app and shared a few dinners with, Lauren. I'm a sovereign of a kingdom with the accompanying responsibilities and protocols that need to be observed. I'm not going to engage in a wait-and-see game while you weigh your options. In this matter, your choices are unfortunately limited.'

'You say unfortunately as if you mean it? And yet I don't believe you're sorry about it at all.'

He shrugged. 'I'm choosing to be practical about it.'

Practical. Protocol. Inconsequential.

Words that sharpened into little arrows and pierced vulnerable places she didn't even know were unprotected until they found their target.

Rising, she put more distance between them, whirling away to squeeze her eyes shut. Then, resenting the show of weakness, she pivoted right back to face him. 'My future choices are mine to make, not yours.'

Disappointment and another indecipherable emotion flashed through his eyes. 'Is what I'm offering you really that deplorable? Is becoming my queen such a nightmare for you?'

My queen.

The title attempted to wrap itself around her heart. She refused to allow it. He didn't love her. So she forced a shrug. 'This wasn't how I saw my life going.'

Again that flash of emotion. 'Life rarely plays out the way we envision.'

'That's not true for you though, is it? You're exactly where you want to be, aren't you?'

Slowly he advanced to where she stood. The folded arms dropped to his sides. He didn't reach for her, but he didn't need to. Her entire being was focused on him.

'Do you think you could've conceived my child, Lauren?' The words were low, deep, throbbing with a kind of possessiveness that warned that, should she answer in the affirmative, life as she knew it would be over.

She could've prevaricated. Or simply refused to answer.

'I'm within my ovulation window. But that means nothing. Unfortunately for you, you can't control things this time, Tahir. And as to whether I want to be your queen, whether I'm carrying your child or not, the answer is no.'

The answer is no.

In the short space of time between realising his blunder with protection and reaching her, Tahir's imagination had gone on a wild rampage.

He'd imagined Lauren's belly round with his child.

He'd imagined holding his child for the first time.

He'd imagined doing things differently. Better. To stop the sins of the father being visited upon the son.

Because...

Every child deserves to be told they're loved...

Those words especially, said with wide, earnest eyes, had drilled into his very soul. Had made him believe...in those frantic minutes...that he might have what it took. That, decades from now, no child of his would confess to another human being that his or her father didn't love them. Instead, they would boast of his affection. They would go through life secure in his unconditional love.

Damn it, Lauren had made him *hope* again. And this time the fall would be greater...because he loved her.

While she...

Whether I'm carrying your child or not...

Tahir couldn't even summon the power to be furious at her. He had absolutely no one to blame but himself.

'Did you hear me?' she bit out, her face still pale from his news. His *unwanted* news.

'Oh, yes, *habibti*. I heard you.'

Did she now flinch at his endearment? When she'd shuddered with delight at it a mere two hours ago? Extracting himself from the wall, he tugged the shroud over the depleted hourglass and set the tray before her.

Startled eyes rose to his. 'What are you doing?'

I don't know. But I can't bear this to end yet. 'We're not done.'

She opened her mouth and every sinew in his body strained for her next words. Because the hope she'd awakened refused to die. But all she said was, 'Fine. Have it your way.'

Her hand shook as she spun the tray.

Lauren knew he'd seen but she didn't care. He was determined to finish his game and she wasn't going to give him the satisfaction of begging him to release her from it.

But even as she went through with the sham of finishing a game that no longer mattered, her other hand dropped beneath the table to her belly.

Pregnant.

A baby… *Tahir's baby* could be growing inside her right this minute. She swallowed, the enormity of that possibility shaking through her. She'd come off the pill after swearing off dating following her thirtieth birthday. And the idea of having sex with Tahir on her arrival in Jukrat had been nigh on laughable.

A wave of dizziness swept over her, making her squeeze her eyes shut once more.

'The prospect of finishing our game is deplorable to you now, too?' he grated.

She wanted to scream and demand why he was bothering. Lauren knew she was a glutton for punishment where this man was concerned because even now, when self-preservation urged her to end this, to flee far and hide, she remained seated. She reached for the silk shroud to her left and tugged it free.

'Ninety minutes between us. That should be enough time,' Tahir said, then turned to walk away.

'Enough time for what?' she asked, the sensation of being in an alternate universe hitting hard.

He stopped, turned. In the shadows thrown by the lamplight, all she saw was his stony expression and eyes that continued to burn far too ferociously. 'You want to be free of me, don't you? You yearn to return home? You'll get your wish soon enough.'

That was how Lauren found herself in the helicopter one hour before midnight, with Tahir beside her and the hourglass counting down between them. They'd barely spoken, each wrapped up in their thoughts.

Uppermost in hers was the fact that the thing she'd dreaded had come true far too quickly. Tahir was getting rid of her. And she didn't think she could bear it.

She pursed her lips tighter, terrified she would blurt out her feelings and damn herself for ever.

When Tahir answered a call a short time into their flight, she was relieved. Then her heart was breaking all over again at the thought that soon she wouldn't hear his voice. Wouldn't experience the dexterity of his brilliant mind or feast her eyes on his towering magnificence.

She would be returning to a half-life not of her parents' making but of a love unrequited. When blurry lights winked beyond the window, she thought it was rain. Then she realised her tears blocked her vision.

She blinked them away as the aircraft set down on the same helipad they'd taken off from yesterday.

The same aide approached, and if he was surprised that his King had returned just a day after leaving, he didn't show it.

Bodyguards didn't bar her way this time. In fact, she was—to her amazement—treated to the same reverent greetings as Tahir. It was probably why she didn't fully take note of her surroundings until she was led into another lavish living room.

And she came face to face with her parents.

'Mum? Dad? What are you doing here?'

'Your mother told me about your conversation,' her father replied, his voice just short of a sneer. 'It was clear you were getting nowhere, and Matt needed us to be here. But we didn't quite think we would be meeting you here.' He sent a puzzled glance at Tahir.

Lauren ignored the puzzling last response and addressed the main one. 'So you came to light a fire under my feet because I wasn't moving fast enough for your liking?'

He stiffened in surprise, then annoyance.

Yes, this was the first time she'd used a less than cordial tone with him. She could excuse herself with the overwhelming emotions coursing through her. But regardless of the circumstance, this conversation was long overdue.

'You look pale. Are you quite all right?' her father said, after a quick, pandering glance at Tahir.

Lauren wanted to laugh but she was mildly terrified she would drown in hysterics. She swiped her hand across her eyes, praying for strength. 'No, I'm not all right. I haven't slept for more than an hour in the last day, and you turning up here because you think I'm...' She stopped to swallow the surge of emotion in her throat. 'You know what? I don't care any more.'

Her mother gasped, her eyes widening before turning cool with disapproval. 'That's hardly the way to talk to your father, Lauren.'

'Oh, no? How about the way you talk to me? The way you treat me?'

Charles cast another glance at Tahir as if gauging his reaction to her outburst. 'I'm not sure what's up with you, but this is hardly the place. Perhaps His Majesty might give us a private—'

'No. He stays. This concerns him, after all, doesn't it? Don't you want to know how I got on with trying to convince him to help Matt?'

'Well, we were told our presence would hasten things. Although we were under the impression that His Majesty was arranging for Matt's lawyer to meet us at our hotel, not be brought here.'

She frowned. Tahir had arranged this?

Her gaze swung to him. He stood with his hands tucked behind his back, his profile formidable as he watched her father. 'You'll be taken to where you need to be in due course,' he said. 'First, you need to finish this conversation with your daughter.'

'You should know I wasn't successful,' Lauren said bluntly. 'Tahir isn't going to step in. My presence here changed nothing. Matt's on his own.' She sensed Tahir stiffen but kept her gaze trained on her parents. 'And so am I.' Something cracked open within her then, but, amazingly, what was left behind wasn't as awful and devastating as she'd feared.

Her father frowned. 'So are you? What does that mean?'

'It means my days of lessening myself for you are over. I resign.' She switched her gaze to her mother. 'And I'll be moving out as soon as I get home. I'm grateful that you gave me a home, but I can't…' She stopped and cleared her throat, bunching her fists so she wouldn't shake so much. 'I'd rather have no love than conditional indifference.'

'This is all absurd. Are you sure the desert heat hasn't got to you? Look, let's settle this properly when you're back—'

'I've never been clearer, Dad.'

His face went florid, his eyes colder than she'd ever seen them. 'I always knew you were an ungrateful child. After all we've done for you—'

'Does that include encouraging her to betray those she cares about? Consistently taking your other child's side instead of hers? What about emotionally blackmailing your own child, Winchester? I don't think that's quite in the parenting manual,' Tahir said.

Lauren's shocked gaze swung back to him. He didn't love her, and yet he was defending her? Was he trying to make it impossible for her heart to ever forget him? 'Tahir, you don't have to—'

Tahir's nostrils flared and she spotted mild rebuke in his eyes before he shifted his attention back to her father. 'Yes, I do. What your father forgot to say was that when I arranged yesterday to have them brought here, he tried the same tactic with me, believing I could be manipulated. Now you're here, perhaps you can elaborate on your intentions?'

Her shocked gaze swung back to her father. 'You really thought you could manipulate Tahir? Don't you know that my desire to have a better relationship with you was your only leverage over me? That I sacrificed…' She stopped unwilling to bare the true state of her tattered heart in front of Tahir, the man who'd decimated it.

Her father squirmed, and his mouth gaped but no words emerged. No words to dispute anything she'd said. Or even attempt to heal her heartache. Foolish tears brimmed in her eyes and she dashed them away.

After a minute, her father pressed his lips shut and shook his head.

'It's time for you to leave,' Tahir decreed, his tone stone-cold.

Charles Winchester nodded after casting a chilling look at Lauren.

With a flick of his hand, Tahir's aide stepped forward. Within seconds, her parents were gone.

She turned on Tahir. 'You arranged this! You wanted it to happen, didn't you?'

He shrugged. 'Yes, I did.'

She couldn't even summon the temper to grit her teeth. All her emotions were locked into the *why, why, why*?

'Men like your father respond predictably to one thing—power. He thought me summoning him meant he could manipulate some out of me. He discovered differently.'

'So this was all another game to you?'

His gaze hardened. 'No, it wasn't. I wanted you to be free of them once and for all.'

'Why? What do you care?'

He stiffened as if she'd knifed him with the words. 'You still don't get it, do you? I can stand many things, but not watching you live a half-life. You needed to take back your power.'

'And that's all it comes down to, is it? Who holds the most power?'

His chin lifted and he cast her a look so pitying she shrivelled where she stood. 'Don't disparage it. Without it, you wouldn't be here. You love what it can do for you. Once upon a time, you lobbied for it because you knew what it could do for the causes you upheld. And admit it, you love it moving between your legs when I take you.'

Heat and cold drenched her. 'It didn't do me a lot of good in the long run, though, did it? Just in case it wasn't clear before, I heard what you said about not helping Matt. About me.'

Regret flashed in his eye and his jaw tightened. But in the next instant, it was gone. 'That's unfortunate. But it's not why you're running back to London. You've already washed your hands of your brother. As for what you overheard, perhaps you shouldn't take things like that at face value.'

Before she could ask what he meant, he was walking away. He returned moments later with the hourglass tray.

'What are you doing? Our twenty-four hours is over. I'm leaving.'

'Not quite. Midnight approaches. Spin the tray one last time, Lauren.'

'Why? What does it matter any more?'

His eyes blazed and this time something contained in them set her insides alight. 'Because I want my life to begin, Lauren. I want *our* lives to begin.'

'I…what do you mean…our lives?'

His nostrils flared and for the first time in a very long time, he seemed at a loss for words. At a loss, full stop. But his eyes…oh, God, his eyes devoured her. In a way that siphoned all of her breath. Risked dampening down the righteous anger she should be fanning—

No.

'You know what? It doesn't matter what you mean—'

'Doesn't it?' Soft words, no less ground-shaking for their impact. 'You've freed yourself from the shackles of conditional love. Don't you want to fight for what you truly want now?'

'Tahir.'

Those eyes burnished brighter. 'I believe you when you say you didn't wish for things to unfold and end the way they did. So do the present and future not really *matter*?'

'I can't…they can't.'

'Why not?'

'You know why not. I'm—'

'If you call yourself a nobody one more time, I'll commission my best architect in Jukrat to build a dungeon just to throw you in until you come to your senses,' he promised through gritted teeth.

Her head snapped up, a little bit of that anger igniting to life. 'I wasn't going to call myself a nobody. I am somebody. I'm my own person. That person is a realist. This…whatever is going on between us…it's a fairy tale. I've woken up. You need to wake up too.'

His chest expanded on a deep breath, his jaw softening a touch. The flames in his eyes morphed. No less powerful but deeper. The kind that promised to burn brighter. Longer. Eternally? 'There she is. The woman who owned me even before I ever clapped eyes on her. The woman no other has ever been able to hold a candle to.'

She gasped. 'Tahir.'

His fist curled hard as if he was physically restraining himself from reaching for her, from acting on the possessive need surging like rip tides in his eyes. 'You keep saying my name like that and I won't be responsible for my actions. We need to clear this up once and for all because I never want to revisit it again.'

Warmth rushed at her, threatening to overwhelm the cold loneliness. But could she trust it? She shook her head. 'Did you not hear what I just said? This isn't real. It can't be. You went from preparing to say goodbye to me in a matter of hours to asking me to be your queen. And you know what changed within those hours? The tiniest possibility that I might be pregnant. Tell me why I shouldn't think it was a knee-jerk reaction triggered by the need to claim your child. Tell me how that's not another form of conditional possession that makes me surplus to requirements?'

'It wasn't,' he answered, his voice as deep as the earth's crust and just as unshakable. 'Do you want to know the first time I imagined you wearing my crown?' he challenged again. He took a single step towards her then froze again. 'I knew within a minute of meeting you twelve years ago that you were exceptional. Bold and unafraid and so damned alive, I couldn't not fall under your spell.' He took a long, deep breath. 'More than the sex and the conversation and the giving heart I knew you possessed, you gave me hope. Made me believe I could be a better version of myself, a better version for the woman I wanted to be my queen, even back then. That hope...that spell hasn't waned, Lauren.'

She shook her head again. 'That's just it, don't you see? Spells by their very definition don't last for ever! We put ourselves in a pressure cooker of twenty-four hours. You'll be a fool to believe it'll be sustainable beyond—'

'Beyond what? Twenty-four hours? Twelve years? A lifetime? I'm prepared to test it. Are you?' he dared.

'No! I can't... I won't do that to you.'

He exhaled harshly. 'Why not? Why are you so hell-bent on saving me from this perceived path you think will lead to misery?'

'Because I...' She froze. Her throat locked tight. She wanted to squeeze her eyes shut, pretend his eyes weren't blazing at her. That he wasn't closing the gap between them, leaving her no room to escape her thoughts. Her very real, far too potent emotions that shook every cell in her being.

'Because you what, *habibti*?' he crooned softly, his breath washing over her forehead as he leaned close, fusing his essence with hers.

When she shook her head, her eyes wide open because, self-preservation be damned, she wasn't going to miss a moment of this, the tiniest self-deprecating smile kicked up the corner of his velvet-smooth lips before he was all purpose and danger again.

Before his lips were caressing her face, lingering on her lips, taking another breath before he said, 'I'll go first, shall I?' He didn't wait for her response. Every muscle in his body was set on one purpose. 'Personally, I think twelve years is more than enough. Don't you? I regret, deeply, that most of it was wasted being bitter and unforgiving and far too invested in feeling aggrieved. Believing the future you hoped for has been taken away from you for ever has a way of doing that to a man.'

Lauren knew her mouth was gaping but she couldn't quite bring herself to correct herself. Tahir didn't seem to mind though. The ferocious look in his eyes didn't abate one little bit.

'I told you that my family lawyers took care of shutting down most of the tabloids within weeks of what happened. What I tried to say back in the desert tonight was that there was nothing to forgive because *I* should've acted differently too. I had the palace PR machine and a team of investigators I could've used to discover the real truth. But I let my father deal with it. I marinated in my bitterness to justify everything that was done to me when I knew deep down you weren't capable of such duplicity. For that, we lost a dozen years. I didn't need a year to know the kind of ruler I would be. Or that those months with you were special. My deepest regret through it all was being separated from you.'

That crack came again, sharper. Harder. And again it was replaced by something stronger. Durable. The everlasting kind that said it wouldn't break or be subject to conditions or whims. It was so overwhelming, tears filled her eyes. 'Oh, God. I can't believe... Tahir.'

He closed the gap, finally. Brushed her tears away with his thumbs before lowering his head to kiss them away. 'No tears. Never again. Stay with me,' he pleaded.

The possibility that this was a dream she'd wake up from soon rendered her speechless. 'I...'

'I know you want to return to London, but give me a chance to show you the best of Jukrat? To make a home here with me? We can spend part of the year in London if you truly miss it...'

Her eyes widened. 'You'd do that for me?'

'For the chance to build a life with triple the happiness we've denied ourselves all these years? I'd do just about anything, *habibti*.'

Hope threatened to soar but, like him, she'd endured having it dashed to grasp it. 'Am I truly your beloved, Tahir?'

The expression that came over his face threatened to blow her away. 'I know what you heard me say about you and about Matt didn't do me any favours, but it was just for my cousin's sake. I instructed Ali to speak to the prosecutor the moment we got to the riad. Your brother has been given another month to prepare his case.'

She gasped. 'Tahir... I don't know what to say.'

His large hands framed her face, his eyes fervid on hers. 'Then listen. There was only ever you, my heart. I want you whether you're carrying our child or not. I want you beside me, ruling our people, dazzling me with that brilliant mind, stunning my senses with your incredible body. I want it all, Lauren. Do you?' he demanded thickly. Ferociously.

She threw her arms around him. 'Yes. Oh, please, yes!'

When she strained towards him, eager for his kiss, he held her back. 'And? Is there something you want to say to me, my heart?' The question was cocky, bordering on imperious, but the vulnerable look in his eyes said he wasn't sure she felt the same. Wasn't sure of the solidity of the ground beneath his feet.

She vowed then that she would never give him cause to doubt her love.

'I love you, Tahir. I've loved you from the moment we met. I loved you even when I thought you hated me, and I'll love you triple hard now I know it's returned. Please, please, let's build that life you promised together?'

He kissed her then. A deep, soul-shaking, life-affirming kiss that began to restore all the broken cracks of deprived affection they'd suffered.

When they parted, she placed his hand on her belly. 'I've learned not to wish for much because it may be denied me. But I wish with everything that I have that this is true. That I'm carrying our child.'

She'd thought it impossible that his eyes could blaze brighter. But in that moment, they did. Dropping to his knees, the Sheikh of Jukrat placed a soft, reverent kiss on her belly.

Then, the most beautiful eyes in the world gazed up at her, love burning deep and true.

'I'm the King. If I will it, it will be so.'

EPILOGUE

One year later

I⟨T⟩ TURNED OUT that they had made a baby together that night in the desert.

Crown Prince Malik Al-Jukrat came screaming into the world nine months later, to his parents' utter joy and the kingdom's jubilation. He didn't care that he'd put his mother through thirty-six hours of labour and his father through bouts of feverish cursing and making promises to every deity he could name.

He was adorable and that was all that mattered.

'If you stare at him with any more adoration, he'll become even more unbearable. And I have plans for those fingers you're letting him wrapped his around so tightly,' Lauren joked as her husband rocked their son beneath the nursery window overlooking the royal gardens.

She'd just finished feeding him in time for his debut at his christening. Like their royal wedding and her coronation as Queen Lauren, Sheikha of Jukrat, Humanitarian Ambassador to the United Nations, the guest list for Malik's christening had grown from several hundred to thousands. Lauren's complaint had been met with an implacable response. One Tahir now liked to trot out every time they hosted a state function or even a private party.

'You're the love of my life. I can't let a day go by without showing the world what a beautiful treasure I've found. Don't deny me.'

And truly, what was a girl to say to that level of adoration? She lapped it up, of course. And because it did her heart good, she gave it back tenfold.

She approached the two loves of her life now, dropping a kiss on her son's head before peering up at Tahir.

His blinding smile awaited her, followed by a kiss that she felt all the way to her toes.

'Does everything look ready?' she said, glancing into the garden where the palace decorators had gone to town with the event planning. Boldly coloured chairs and flowers were spread out in cosy groupings, inviting guests to mingle. Lauren had taken inspiration from Tahir's desert home—their desert home—and the result was breathtaking and relaxing.

'They will be unless they want to incur Maman's wrath,' Tahir responded dryly.

As if on cue, the decorator and event planners rushed into view, trailing an older woman dressed in the sort of stylish French elegance that shrieked her royalty. She tossed out instructions, her hands flicking left and right as she navigated the decorations.

Lauren grinned. 'She thrives on occasions like these, doesn't she? She's already planning Malik's first birthday party.'

Far from discarding Lauren's urge to look deeper into his mother's behaviour and how it'd dictated his relationship with her, Tahir had taken it to heart. A quick detour via Paris on their way back from their honeymoon in Zanzibar had laid the groundwork for a new relationship. His mother's confession that the lump sums paid to her had been at her father's instigation and that he wouldn't take no for an answer had led her to believe that was the relationship he wished her to have with his children. She hadn't been proud of it, but she'd reasoned that a skewed relationship was better than none at all.

Tahir's scepticism had eroded with continued contact, and Malik's arrival had finally brought about a complete change of heart. Malik's grandmother adored him and wasn't afraid to show it one little bit.

'Any thawing from Javid?'

Her brother-in-law hadn't been receptive to Tahir's urgings to renew *his* relationship with his mother. In fact, they'd had a heated row about it.

'He'll come around in his own time,' Tahir said. His gaze drifted to the far side of the grounds where Javid paced while on a phone call. The problems with the trade agreements had taken longer to fix in Riyaal, a fact Javid grumbled about every chance he got. Her brother-in-law had moaned at dinner last night that he hadn't had a girlfriend in months, a fact Lauren had warned him not to remedy at his nephew's party.

His grin and I-Make-No-Promises response had filled her with dread.

'Or he'll find a woman half as incredible as my wife and she'll help him embrace every aspect of love, as I have.'

She blinked back sappy tears, even as she teased, 'Only half as incredible?'

Tahir's tawny gaze burned into hers. 'No one holds a candle to you, my heart. They can try, but no one ever will. It's why I'm grateful every single day for you. For the life you've given me and the love I'll cherish for ever.'

She rose on tiptoes and pressed her lips to his, uncaring that tears streamed down her face and she was ruining her make-up.

'As I'll cherish you too, Tahir. For ever.'

* * * * *